HELP ME

(A Katie Winter FBI Suspense Thriller—Book 5)

Molly Black

Molly Black

Bestselling author Molly Black is author of the MAYA GRAY FBI suspense thriller series, comprising nine books (and counting); the RYLIE WOLF FBI suspense thriller series, comprising six books (and counting); of the TAYLOR SAGE FBI suspense thriller series, comprising three books (and counting); and of the KATIE WINTER FBI suspense thriller series, comprising six books (and counting).

An avid reader and lifelong fan of the mystery and thriller genres, Molly loves to hear from you, so please feel free to visit www.mollyblackauthor.com to learn more and stay in touch.

BOOKS BY MOLLY BLACK

MAYA GRAY MYSTERY SERIES
GIRL ONE: MURDER (Book #1)
GIRL TWO: TAKEN (Book #2)
GIRL THREE: TRAPPED (Book #3)
GIRL FOUR: LURED (Book #4)
GIRL FIVE: BOUND (Book #5)
GIRL SIX: FORSAKEN (Book #6)
GIRL SEVEN: CRAVED (Book #7)
GIRL EIGHT: HUNTED (Book #8)
GIRL NINE: GONE (Book #9)

RYLIE WOLF FBI SUSPENSE THRILLER
FOUND YOU (Book #1)
CAUGHT YOU (Book #2)
SEE YOU (Book #3)
WANT YOU (Book #4)
TAKE YOU (Book #5)
DARE YOU (Book #6)

TAYLOR SAGE FBI SUSPENSE THRILLER
DON'T LOOK (Book #1)
DON'T BREATHE (Book #2)
DON'T RUN (Book #3)

KATIE WINTER FBI SUSPENSE THRILLER
SAVE ME (Book #1)
REACH ME (Book #2)
HIDE ME (Book #3)
BELIEVE ME (Book #4)
HELP ME (Book #5)
FORGET ME (Book #6)

PROLOGUE

Stephanie Grant walked downstairs, shivering, making sure the light was on before she headed into the shadowy hall. The cold, blowing downpour was only part of the reason why she felt spooked. She'd woken from a troubled dream this morning, and in the early hours she'd been sure she heard screaming coming from somewhere. A fight, perhaps? Or maybe just a few wild youths headed home after the bars had closed?

She was living in this rental in downtown Vancouver while saving for her own place, but she was wondering if it would be better to give up on that dream and look for a house-share out in the suburbs. She didn't enjoy city living, and she felt uneasy at the thought of the eight-block walk to work in the rainy predawn.

There seemed to be strange things happening in the area. Mel, her co-worker, had mentioned yesterday that she'd thought she was being followed when she left the bakery. She'd actually taken a different route home to make sure of avoiding the guy. And there had been a few muggings in neighboring streets recently. A few robberies.

Maybe that was the reason for her nightmare, Stephanie wondered.

Grabbing her umbrella from the stand in the hall, and pulling her jacket tight around her, she gritted her teeth, stepping out into the blowing darkness.

She was looking forward to the warmth of the baker's kitchen, and making a start on the day's breads and rolls, which would need to be ready by the time her first early morning customers started arriving.

Hurrying across the road, she noticed a broken bottle on the sidewalk, the glass glinting dimly in the streetlight.

The memory of last night's screaming surfaced in her mind again. Teens, maybe. Rowdy and drunk, throwing things as they walked. That was all, she reassured herself.

Vancouver's streets were still dark, the buildings silent. The only sounds were the gusting wind, the hiss of rain, and the distant rumble of traffic from the bridge.

The wind had risen, blowing the rain in sheets across the street. She clutched her coat tight and her umbrella close, ducking her head as she hurried through the storm.

Most days she didn't mind the walk. And in summer she liked to see the way the city came to life as the sun rose. The shutters opening, the blinds pulled up, restaurants and shops getting ready to greet the growing crowds.

But not today.

The late-winter weather was too oppressive, the rain blinding. A few early drivers were out, headlights washing over the sidewalk and walls, shining on the puddles.

In the distance she heard the high wail of a siren.

She glanced behind her, wondering if there was someone following her. She thought she'd heard splashing footsteps, but when she looked, nobody was there.

Turning back, she slipped on the wet sidewalk and almost fell. Stumbling and catching herself against a wall, she listened.

No movement. No sounds. Maybe it had just been the rain and wind.

She hurried across the intersection, her boots splashing in the water, and turned the corner.

As she reached the street where the bakery was located, she shivered. From the cold, from the dream, and from the feeling that she wasn't alone. She turned, looking back over the road, the lights and traffic and blowing rain.

But there was nothing to see.

She frowned, thinking about the dream. And the feeling of being watched by someone. Then she turned and walked on.

There, at last, was the cheerful pink and white sign of the bakery. She felt a sense of relief that this oddly disturbing journey to work was over at last. Only a few more moments and she would be safely inside.

But then, crossing the road, she frowned. The light of the sign above illuminated something ahead of her, something strange and dark, in the shade of the overhang.

Stephanie felt a chill go through her. What was it?

It had been trash bag collection yesterday. This looked like a discarded trash bag. She moved forward, looking nervously and suspiciously at the dark form in the shadows just outside the open back door of the bakery.

Her heart accelerated.

It wasn't a trash bag.

She could see two legs, in dark stockings and black velvet boots, in the shadows. And a pale, outflung hand streaked with blood.

Clapping her hand over her mouth to stifle a scream, Stephanie realized the awful, impossible truth.

"No," she whispered. "No, no, no!"

It was Mel lying there. Her colleague. Yesterday, she'd been sure she was being followed. This morning, she was dead.

Stephanie had no idea what had happened, but she could see a dark crimson pool beneath her and as her shocked mind processed what it must be, she screamed aloud. This had been violent. Mel had been attacked.

Shrieking in horror, unable to believe what she was seeing, Stephanie backed away, fumbling for her phone, turning as she grabbed it to run. She wasn't waiting here to call 911. Not when Mel had been killed, just a few minutes ago.

She fled across the street, her breath sobbing in her lungs, fear overwhelming her. She wanted to hide away and never come back here, ever.

Why had Mel been targeted? Why?

And then an even worse thought loomed in her mind.

What if this killer was still lurking somewhere nearby, waiting for her?

CHAPTER ONE

Katie Winter sighed in frustration as she did the ritual early morning check of her emails to see if the details on her sister's case were available yet. Why had no information come through, she anxiously wondered. Even though the missing person's case was fifteen years old, Katie couldn't help feeling that every moment counted now in reviewing it.

"Why is there nothing yet?" she muttered to herself, tapping her fingers on the wooden table.

She was sitting in the dining room of her apartment in Sault Ste. Marie, on the North American side of the cross-border town where the task force she worked for as a special investigator was based. Her bedroom was quiet and cozy, but the lounge-dining room area had the view she'd grown to love, overlooking the St. Mary's River.

Staring out at the calming view, Katie reminded herself that reopening a cold case was not a quick process, especially when the previous records had been archived before digitization had become the norm. It involved seemingly endless time lags and delays before all the evidence and statements could be in front of her.

But for Katie, the wait felt unbearable. She longed to know what had really happened, back on that fateful day when her sixteen-year-old twin had disappeared. She felt impatient to read through the witness reports, the timeline, and to understand exactly what had really played out during the riverside search. During that search, the police had not found Josie, but had arrested the serial killer Charles Everton, who'd been in the exact location where Josie's kayak had capsized.

But with no emails in her inbox, she would need to be patient for longer.

At that moment, Katie's phone began ringing, providing a welcome distraction.

Standing up from her chair, she rushed through to her bedroom, where her phone was still on charge, to take the call. As it was not yet seven a.m., she imagined that it was likely to be Scott, who headed up the cross-border task force, calling with a new case.

When she looked down at her phone, she saw it was from a number she recognized, but had not expected to hear from.

The number was for Northfields Prison in New York State. This was where Charles Everton was serving a life sentence for multiple murders. She thought it was a weird coincidence that just a moment ago, he'd been in her thoughts.

The week before last, Katie had been allowed a brief meeting with Everton in the prison. During the meeting, he'd threatened her, and combined with his other infractions over the past few days, he had been sent to solitary.

What had happened, she wondered, feeling anxious about the possibilities. Had he escaped? Had he died? Something important must have occurred for the prison to be calling her now.

Quickly she took the call.

"Is that FBI Agent Katie Winter?" a man's voice asked.

"Speaking," she said.

She grabbed the phone off the charger and walked back to her laptop, which was set up on the dining room table, feeling nervous and expectant as she waited for the caller to say more.

"It's Mike Beach here, head warden at Northfields Prison."

This was sounding like something had happened, Katie feared, with a twist of her stomach.

"Morning, Mike. How can I help?" she asked.

"Charles Everton has requested to meet with you."

The statement was as shocking as a bucket of ice water in the face.

To meet? With her?

The man she suspected of murdering Josie, who'd stonewalled and taunted and refused to answer her questions in their last meeting, was now wanting to see her again?

"Agent Winter? Are you there?" Beach asked.

In her shock, she'd been too stunned to reply.

"Yes, I'm here. I'm just surprised by this," she admitted.

"Surprised? I admit I was myself," Beach said. "I can understand your reaction. But he was very clear that he wants to see you again. And I have to say, he was insistent."

"Is Everton currently in solitary?" Katie asked, to clarify the situation.

"Yes. And he'll be there another week at least," Beach reminded her. "We are not shortening his time in solitary because he wants to meet with you. We considered this might be a tactic he was using to get out early."

"I'm glad you decided on that," Katie said, also not wanting Everton to use her as a way of cutting short his punishment term.

"He has been fully informed that he is going to complete the full term in solitary, and that requesting this meeting is not going to shorten his term, nor will it prevent any extension of the term, or any future stints in solitary, should his behavior warrant it."

"Good," Katie said, feeling confident that they were taking the hardest possible line with this dangerous prisoner.

"But he still wants to meet with you once he is back in the maximum security cells."

The last time she'd seen him, the man had been utterly hostile and unremorseful. But his behavior had gone a step too far and earned him a punishment that even this psychopathic man had dreaded. Everton had been horrified about going to solitary. He clearly didn't do well in that environment. Perhaps being locked up alone for a stretch had given him a chance to reconsider, or even repent having taken such a hard line with her.

Did she dare to hope so?

"And you're okay with this?" Katie asked. "With me meeting him again?"

"Are you?" Beach asked. "If you're okay with it, then when the time is right, I'll schedule it in, and let you know."

A tingling sense of excitement began racing up her spine.

"Yes. Yes, I am okay with it," Katie said. "Thank you for calling and letting me know."

"I'll be in touch," Beach said.

Katie cut the call. Her mind was racing. This was a completely unexpected turn of events.

Everything she'd heard about Everton had made it clear that he was not a man to change his mind. He had no compassion or empathy. He was a psychopath who was unrepentant and considered himself above the law and beyond any mercy.

And yet, Everton had not only requested their next meeting, he'd pleaded for it.

That had to mean something.

6

Katie hoped that she would learn more about the disturbing circumstances that had surrounded her sister's disappearance, more than fifteen years ago.

She was desperate to piece together what had really happened on that fateful day of the kayaking accident. Reopening the case would provide one piece of the puzzle, and re-interviewing Everton might provide another. After all, he definitely had been in the exact area when Josie had disappeared. That was concrete fact, and why the police search had picked him up.

Two and a half weeks in solitary confinement, she imagined, was long enough for a criminal to be desperate to talk to anyone in the outside world, even if it meant admitting to the most heinous acts.

She just hoped that this time she'd be able to fight her way through his defenses and discover what he knew.

If he knew anything at all.

She was determined to take whatever chance she was given, and she started mentally working out how she could fit in the time to travel to the prison and talk to him again. It wasn't going to be easy, that was certain, especially with her unpredictable case load.

Plus, this incident was so far in the past. Katie sighed, wishing that at the time she hadn't been sixteen, with little knowledge of investigation procedures, and totally traumatized by her own irresponsible decision to have headed out on the water when the rapids were too dangerous. If only she'd been able to investigate and search at the time, instead of being confined to the house in disgrace. Could she somehow have saved Josie's life if she had?

That was something Katie thought about often, but always with the same twist of guilt.

It was entirely possible Everton had not only been there when the kayak flipped, but that he might know what had happened to her sister.

She knew she should be wary about her hope for this meeting. After all, there was no guarantee that Everton would talk to her. He might have some other game in mind.

But, at that moment, her phone rang again.

Katie grabbed it immediately, seeing that this time it was her boss, Detective Scott, on the line.

Without a doubt, this meant that a new case had landed. She would be reunited with her investigation partner Leblanc, after he'd been out of town for a few days, and they would face this challenge together.

Picking up the call, she wondered, with adrenaline surging, what it would involve.

CHAPTER TWO

Detective Leblanc glanced down at his phone, which was ringing as he walked onto the airplane. To his surprise, he saw it was a police colleague of his calling from Paris.

Leblanc guessed that this old friend had heard about the career opportunity he'd been offered, and was calling to find out if he was taking it.

"Bonjour," he answered, feeling conflicted all over again about the decision.

A couple of weeks ago, he'd decided not to apply for the senior detective job in Paris, and to remain with the task force. But Leblanc had underestimated the power of his own thoughts and feelings.

His heart was begging him to stay with the cross-border task force, but his head was pleading with him to grasp this career opportunity, to return to the city where he'd spent most of his working life, and to benefit from everything it might bring.

Potential revenge was high on the list, and Leblanc found himself unable to get these thoughts out of his head.

While he'd been in Paris, his investigation partner and lover, Celeste, had been murdered by a prison inmate, Hugo Gagnon. Celeste's murder had destroyed Leblanc's life. He had never forgotten, and never forgiven, what Gagnon had done. He longed for him to get the punishment he deserved. Life in prison was too good for him.

"Bonjour, Leblanc," his colleague said. "I am calling you with some interesting information that I just found out."

"What is that?" Leblanc asked, feeling curious as he filed to his seat.

"Do you know the situation with Gagnon?" he asked in a hushed voice.

"What is it?" Now Leblanc felt eager to learn more.

"Don't say I told you, but there is a possibility he will be transferred. From the maximum-security prison where he is now, to another one. An older prison, which is not so well managed."

"What does that mean?" Leblanc asked, feeling intrigued.

"Security is very poor there. And there are several inmates in that prison who hate Gagnon. He was part of a gang, before he was arrested. It is common knowledge that if he is transferred, he will be murdered there."

Leblanc couldn't help it, but he deeply longed for Gagnon to get the retribution he deserved - his life for Celeste's.

"How do they decide who gets moved?" he asked. That would be the key to Gagnon's fate - whether he was among the inmates who got moved, or not.

"I will try to find out whose decision it is," his ex-colleague had said. "And whether there is any way of influencing it," he added meaningfully.

"I would appreciate that," Leblanc said. He felt as if a door had opened that he hadn't even known about.

"Please, this must remain confidential. Don't tell anyone I called you," his colleague said.

"I won't," he promised.

As the plane took off, Leblanc realized he had a tough choice ahead of him. If he did learn who was making that decision, would he intervene? Would he plead for Gagnon to be moved, knowing it would be his death sentence? Was his quest for revenge going to take him that far?

Prisoners like Gagnon were not moved often. This opportunity would certainly not happen again.

He sighed, staring down at the snowy landscape as the plane lifted high into the cloudless sky.

It would literally be manipulating a man's life.

He wondered what Katie, his investigation partner for a couple of months now, would think about the fact he was considering this. What would she feel about it, and him?

Would she believe he was no different from Gagnon, and plotting to kill? Leblanc felt his stomach clench. He did not want to be like Gagnon. But, he wanted Gagnon's life more than anything.

Transferring him to the other prison was almost undoubtedly sending him to his death. Would he be able to obtain the power to influence the situation, and if he did get that power, would he use it?

These were very troubling thoughts.

He believed he had finished with his quest for vengeance. Yet, it seemed the prospect of getting Gagnon the punishment he deserved stirred the dark emotions he had buried deep in his soul.

He'd been living a lie. He'd been hoping that in this new town, he was free from the demons of the past. But it seemed not.

The next few days would be tense, no doubt, waiting to see if Gagnon's fate was within his power to decide.

Leaning back in his seat, he closed his eyes. He felt like a stranger to himself.

Should he tell Katie? Should he even discuss it with her, or would she be appalled by what he had been thinking?

And then, he saw that while pondering over the decision ahead, he'd had an incoming message from Scott. His boss knew he was currently on a flight back home.

"We have a new case called in. There seems to be a serial killer at work in the Seattle-Vancouver area. Call me as soon as you land, and be ready to take a connecting flight immediately."

Leblanc felt adrenaline surge through him. This was exactly the challenge that he needed.

He could take his mind off the uncertainty surrounding Gagnon, and focus on the serious case that awaited him. A serial murder investigation would require his full commitment, with no opportunity for distraction. Chasing down a killer could lead to a very dark and risky place, as Leblanc knew.

For the next while, all his time and attention would be on doing whatever it took to catch this murderer.

He felt simultaneously excited and relieved by this, and was looking forward to being partnered with Katie again. He realized how much he'd missed her company while he'd been away. The way she hooked her shiny, brunette hair behind her ears thoughtfully while she looked at case documents. The way her green eyes blazed with excitement when she had a lead, or a breakthrough. Her perception and intuition was phenomenal.

He'd been surprised by how well they had learned to work together, after a rocky start. Now, he felt a real connection to her.

This was something of which he'd not thought himself capable, still feeling so devastated by the death of Celeste. But, even knowing that he was not yet fully recovered, he had to acknowledge that Katie Winter was intelligent and independent, and Leblanc felt drawn to her.

And he had also come to trust her instincts and judgment, which was something he'd not quite expected.

He felt in some ways that they had a lot in common.

At the same time, he knew that such a case could bring great personal danger for both of them. Going into a new case was never easy, especially as he grew closer to his investigation partner.

Leblanc knew his emotions were already entangled in this partnership, far more than they should be for a professional relationship.

He wasn't going to fight it, but it meant that every new case brought an additional level of anxiety for his partner's safety. He'd lost someone he worked closely with and felt for. He did not want this to happen again, ever.

But there was a killer on the loose, and above all else, his investigator's instincts flared. He felt eager to start the hunt, as soon as his plane landed.

CHAPTER THREE

Katie was waiting in the airport lounge at Sault Ste. Marie international airport. She expected Leblanc to join her any minute. They had two hours until they boarded the flight to Seattle, and in that time they were going to be briefed by Scott on what the case involved.

A new case was something that she was more than ready for. She was feeling eager to get started.

There he was. She felt an unexpected skip of her heart as the tall, fit, olive-skinned man entered the lounge and walked over to her, smiling.

"Katie!"

"Leblanc. How was your vacation?" He'd told her he had been spending a few days with his aunt and uncle, who lived near Montreal.

"It was relaxing. Always good to visit family," he said, before making a wry face, as if remembering Katie's circumstances, and adding, "For some at any rate."

She felt grateful for his sympathetic acknowledgement that for her, family was the opposite.

"It's quiet enough here." She'd chosen a seat all the way in the corner of the lounge, which was not busy at this time. "Shall we call Scott now?"

She could see Leblanc was as anxious to get started as she was.

"Let's do that," he agreed.

Katie dialed, and set the phone on speaker, glancing around to make sure they were private. A moment later, Scott answered.

"Leblanc. Winter. Thanks for being able to prepare for this so fast. This is a new case with all the signs of being a suspected serial. There's widespread panic about it. The state governor has pleaded with us to solve it as fast as we can. With two young women targeted so far, and the level of violence involved, it's the worst sort of crime for generating fear. Here's what we know."

Katie waited, feeling expectant, for the details to be set out.

"The first murder occurred three days ago, in Seattle. It was in a park on the city's outskirts. The victim was Amber Morrison, a twenty-five year old legal secretary. It happened after dark, as she was walking back from a friend's house. And as you can see from the photos I'm about to show you, the attacker clearly used a large bladed weapon. A hatchet or an axe. She was struck in the back of the head and would have died almost instantly."

Katie prepared herself, taking a deep breath for steadiness and calmness. Seeing violence was never easy. She hated that anyone had to die in such a way, even though it kindled a flame of resolve inside her to pursue this and find the killer, whatever it took.

She narrowed her eyes as the photos flashed up, taking in the extreme violence of the attack. The only consolation was that, without a doubt, death would have been instant. But what had it taken, physically and mentally, for someone to bring down an axe with such lethal force and murderous intent?

"Yes. That's a deep wound, and looks to have been accurately placed," Leblanc agreed.

"You're right. It's an extremely accurate blow," Katie noted. "Whoever did that was either lucky or skilled."

"Exactly," Scott agreed.

"Any evidence? Any leads?" Katie then asked.

Scott sounded resigned. "There are no cameras near the park. It was probably around eight p.m. People were inside. The park was quiet. She'd been taking a shortcut through, and the people who found her an hour or two later were doing the same. Local police were obviously horrified by the violence of the crime in a peaceful area. The crime shook the neighborhood, but they've been coming up blank in terms of evidence, motives, or any other leads."

"And the second killing?"

"That was called in early this morning," Scott said. "The victim was a thirty-year-old woman called Melany Mason, who worked at a bakery in Vancouver. She was struck in exactly the same way, using a similar weapon, as she arrived to open up for work at about four-thirty a.m. As you can imagine, the fact that the same crime has now occurred in a different city is extremely troubling. This killer is on the move and there's no telling where he or she will strike next."

Again, Katie narrowed her eyes as the images flashed up.

"Now, the notable detail in this killing is that Melany suspected someone was following her the day before. She told her colleague, who later found her body, as much."

"Did she say more? Give a description?"

"No," Scott said. "She just mentioned she'd been aware of it and had chosen a different route home."

Katie made a mental note to question the colleague in detail. Any remembered fragment of information could help.

"And you've established that these two women don't know each other?" Katie asked. "They have nothing in common?"

"No. They have no known acquaintances in common, or shared friends."

"Definitely a serial, then. And as you say, already cross border, which raises serious questions," Katie observed.

"It does. Hopefully you can get some answers soon," Scott agreed.

"Any signatures apart from the method of killing?"

"Nothing we've found so far," Scott replied. "The coroner has indicated that from the angle of the blows, the killer is right handed, and from the height of the blows, probably average to tall in height."

Katie watched as Leblanc nodded, his intense, dark eyes taking in all the information.

She knew he was focusing on trying to figure out who the person was, and where they could be. She felt the same.

"When you land, you're going to meet up with the detective currently handling the Seattle case. His name is Paul Rix. I've been in touch with him to make sure you have all the resources you need. I've worked with him before. He's a good man, and thorough," Scott reassured them.

"That's good," Leblanc agreed.

"I'm counting on you to make quick progress. Let us know what you find."

"I hope we will make progress, and we'll keep you in the loop," Katie said. They cut the call and she looked away for a moment. She wondered if Leblanc would be able to tell that she was a little shaken.

Of course he did.

"You okay?" Leblanc asked, watching her as she struggled to get over the aftershocks of the pictures they'd seen.

It was always difficult seeing murder in all its viciousness, no matter how many times she did.

The hatred that someone must harbor, to do that to a human being who was nothing to them, and had never done them harm, never failed to shake her.

But at the same time, she was also desperate to understand how the killer must be feeling. Difficult as it was to try and tune in to such a flawed, damaged, or psychopathic person, she knew that if she could understand how a killer's mind worked, it would help her catch him.

She could not feel pure hatred but had to feel empathy. Chilling as it was, she had to try and align with his thought processes in order to track who he was.

"I'm good," she acknowledged to Leblanc. "I was just thinking about who this person is, which is always troubling. But we need to think about how he or she is going to behave next. I'm strongly guessing that from the force used, and the weapon used, our killer is a man."

"Yes, I agree with that. The MO definitely points to a male killer, physically and mentally. Why an axe?" Leblanc asked.

"It must be in some way significant to him."

"He might be using a weapon that he is familiar with, has available, and can use well?" Leblanc added.

"Yes. With strength and expertise. But how is he hiding it? You can't walk around town holding an axe. Not unless you're clearly a maintenance person. Worth bearing in mind," Katie said.

Leblanc nodded. "A maintenance person would fit in with the park setting, but not the urban setting near the bakery. That was downtown. But at this stage, we can't say more but must keep it in mind. Perhaps it's a front. Perhaps it's his day job."

Katie continued. "The kill itself is brutal, but accurate. He's efficient. No hesitation with either kill."

"And no attempt to hide the body," Leblanc observed.

"Yes. He's not covering up," she said, thinking it through. "He either doesn't care, or he's proud of what he's doing. Or else, he's too focused on getting away quickly. That also tells us something."

She glanced over at Leblanc, who was looking thoughtful.

"I'm glad you're here," he said. "We're going to catch this guy."

Katie felt relieved at his words. When he'd arrived in the lounge, he appeared to be stressed, and she had wondered if there was anything going on that he wasn't telling her. But now, he seemed intent on the murder investigation and his words reassured her that he was more than focused.

"I'm glad you're here too," she admitted.

Katie could feel her hunter's instincts flaring in her mind as she thought about the case.

The disturbing fact that neither of them had mentioned was the pressure of time. This man had killed twice in the space of a few days. He was on a short interval.

It was a tough burden to have to acknowledge that the next major lead might only come when he killed again.

And that was why getting on the plane, and examining the first crime scene, was hugely important in terms of gathering clues.

"Is that our flight being called?" Leblanc asked.

"It is," Katie said.

She couldn't wait to get to Seattle and start investigating the evidence that might point the way to this killer before he claimed another life.

CHAPTER FOUR

Leblanc headed into the Seattle airport terminal building, walking side by side with Katie. He only vaguely took in the ambiance of the airport, the hugs and greetings, hellos and farewells, a thousand different stories playing out around him.

At this time, he was focused on only one story, which was what had happened to the killer's first victim, Amber Morrison, as she walked through the park after nightfall.

"Detective Rix is here," Leblanc said, glancing down at his phone to confirm the message as they walked. "He's waiting outside in the pick-up zone to take us straight to the crime scene."

"Great," Katie said, checking her watch. "It'll be good to get going on this. It's already noon."

It was a gray day, with light snow threatening. Somber, still and quiet, as if the clouds were smothering the city.

Leblanc looked around for the silver unmarked Ford that Rix had described.

"There it is," he said, and they headed over.

A plainclothes detective with short, sandy hair and a round, intelligent face was sitting in the front seat. He got out and opened the passenger door for them.

"Detective Rix," Leblanc said, shaking his hand.

" Agent Winter and Detective Leblanc?" Rix said, glancing at Katie. "I've heard good things about this cross-border task force. I hope you can make progress on this. It was a shocking crime, and I don't mind admitting, our entire precinct has been in a state of panic trying to figure it out. There's been an outcry about it and we're under immense pressure to provide answers. The fact it's a serial, and he's killed in other cities, makes it even more troubling but it also lets us off the hook in terms of local leads, which we were getting nowhere with."

They climbed into the car. The detective took his place in the front.

"I'm going to drive you straight to the crime scene. I'm sure you'd like to get some perspective on the actual location. Of course, as I've said, we battled with the lack of evidence and suspects. So it's unlikely to offer you any significant findings, but who knows?"

Rix pulled away, leaving the airport and driving fast and efficiently. They were soon heading out of the city, and on the highway going north.

Leblanc knew that the case had already been investigated thoroughly, but as they drove north, he was hoping Rix was right, and that there would be more to be uncovered, no matter how insignificant it seemed. Each detail could be relevant.

"So, what else can you tell us about this case?" he asked Rix, who was driving through the gray afternoon at a steady speed, occasionally using the windshield wipers to remove stray snowflakes or splatters of sleet.

"The victim was Amber Morrison, twenty-five-years-old, a legal secretary. She worked for a suburban law firm, and lived alone. She went to visit a friend on the other side of the park, and I believe they had a couple of drinks. She then walked home, and must have been attacked on the way. The friend is a work colleague, who confirmed she'd left just before eight, and that it had been a regular evening in every way and nothing had seemed to be amiss. They used to get together every few weeks for drinks."

"When was the body found?" Katie asked.

"It was found a couple of hours later, at about a quarter to ten p.m., by two residents who were also cutting through the park after taking a late bus home. They called police immediately and we secured the scene."

Leblanc shook his head, knowing that this already represented a scene where few leads were likely to be found. It had been late, dark and cold, and the time gap in terms of the body being found would have allowed the killer to make an easy getaway.

Rix turned off the highway and began winding his way through a suburb called Greenways. It looked to be a typical family residential area, Leblanc saw. No wonder the community had been shaken. He noticed a few large parks interspersed with the small homes as they drove.

"Was there any sign that the body had been moved? To try to hide it?"

"No. It was obvious that the body had never been moved," Rix said. "She fell forward into the snow, under a tree. The surrounding snow was not been disturbed at all."

"No footprints?" Leblanc asked.

"Unfortunately, the pathway had been swept clear of snow earlier that day and no more had fallen. So there was no sign of footprints at all. We think he must have come up behind her. She was killed shortly after a crossroad in the paths, so he could have been waiting on a side path."

"How about the murder weapon?"

"That was never found," Rix said.

He pulled over outside the low fence of a grassy, treed park with paved paths running through it.

"This is the scene," he said. "Ms. Morrison walked this way. Her friend's house is two blocks to the left. Her home is three blocks further on, to the right of the park. This is the walkway she took."

They set off along the narrow, paved path.

Leblanc was imagining the nighttime scene. He thought about Amber Morrison walking along this same path, perhaps preoccupied or thoughtful, maybe glancing down at her phone to catch up on messages.

"This is where it happened." Rix's words interrupted his thoughts.

Crime scene tape still demarcated the scene as they approached, flapping gently in the chilly breeze. Leblanc saw it was shortly after a cross in the path, and a few yards beyond a bushy cluster of trees. It would have been easy for the killer to spot her and move in, and then to have wielded that axe with devastating force.

He saw Katie glance sadly at a couple of flower arrangements that had been placed on the snow near the tape.

"Her mother and father came here yesterday," Rix said. "They flew in from Chicago."

"How did they seem?" Katie asked.

"Devastated. Like any parent would be. They're still here, sorting out the arrangements for the funeral and memorial service. They weren't particularly close to her and hadn't spoken in the past few days. But Amber's sister, Megan Morrison, lives a few miles away, and spoke to her regularly, so you can question her after we're wrapped up here."

Leblanc was glad they would get that opportunity. They needed to learn more about what was happening in Amber's life, and if she'd been worried or harassed by anyone before her death.

"Can we see the crime scene photos?" Katie asked.

Leblanc nodded, feeling it would be helpful to view them at the actual scene.

Rix opened up a tablet and scrolled through.

"Here's where she was found," he said.

The photos showed Amber lying in the snow, face down, her shoulder-length brunette hair fanned out around her. She wore a dark jacket, a scarf and gloves. The snow around her was stained dark red.

Leblanc looked at the image, feeling the heavy weight of the murder, the sudden shock of a brutal, violent death. An innocent walk through the park, and she had been murdered.

"I know you must have done your best to find forensic evidence. Did you get anything?" Katie asked.

"No. Not a thing."

"How tall was the victim?"

"Five foot six," Rix said.

Leblanc nodded. That was slightly shorter than Katie. But even so, it would have taken height and strength for a killer to bring down that axe with killing force.

"I'm thinking we have to be looking for someone very strong, and fairly tall," Katie echoed his thoughts.

Rix nodded. "Pathologist agrees it was a very accurate downward blow. He raised the axe and brought it down with lethal intent."

"Anyone notice a stranger lurking around? Any unusual people, vehicles, anything?"

Rix shook his head.

"It's a quiet neighborhood; people keep to themselves here. And there are not many cameras, outside of the main roads and some of the stores."

Leblanc was wondering about the logistics of the murder. The killer must have left the scene with a bloodstained axe. He could have taken the weapon with him, or else disposed of it somewhere that it had not yet been found.

Even in one of the ponds. There were a few in the park.

If he'd taken it with him then he would have had to conceal it either in a large bag or some other covering. He would have worn dark clothing, Leblanc thought, to avoid the risk of blood spatter showing.

He was starting to see a picture, but it was frustratingly vague.

"Was there anything else the pathologist noticed or picked up?" Katie asked.

Rix shook his head. "Nothing. No defensive wounds. She was surprised. Killed almost instantly. One lethal axe blow, delivered from a height."

Leblanc shook his head.

"Can we visit the sister now?" he asked.

He hoped that Megan would be able to fill in more details, or background, that could provide a clue to why the killer had chosen her. Leblanc was still hoping to find a connection between the two victims that would point the way to this man's identity.

CHAPTER FIVE

Katie climbed into the passenger seat of Rix's vehicle, wondering if Megan Morrison would be able to provide any insight or clues. She hoped so, because that quiet crime scene, incongruous by its location in such a peaceful neighborhood, was offering nothing for them to take further.

"Megan lives a couple of miles away, closer to downtown," Rix explained as he turned onto the main road. They were driving into town. Traffic was heavier, and so were the snow clouds, closing in for what promised to be a grim afternoon.

The upcoming interview would be tough. Speaking to bereaved relatives was never easy.

She couldn't help thinking that at this time, Amber's family had come together. Josie's disaster had split her own family apart and at no time since then had Katie seen a chance for things to change. She wondered briefly if she would ever be on speaking terms with her parents. She'd recently tried to heal the rift by literally walking into their home and surprising them, but when she'd mentioned Josie, it had all gone disastrously wrong again.

"Here we are," Rix said, pulling up outside a well-kept three-story apartment. "Megan lives on the first floor."

Katie climbed out of the car, breathing in the damp, cold air.

Then she followed Rix to the apartment's lobby, and along the corridor to Megan's home.

Rix knocked, and the door was opened by a pretty brunette with a tear-stained face.

"Megan Morrison? May we come in?" Katie asked gently. "We're from a special investigation unit, looking to get some information on this crime."

Megan nodded and stepped back to let them in. The apartment was spacious and stylish, with an open-plan living area, an exposed brick wall, and an impressive glass-fronted fireplace.

"Please, have a seat." She gestured to one of the two black leather couches.

23

"Thank you for agreeing to speak to us," Leblanc said. "We're sorry for your loss."

They all sat down.

Megan nodded sadly, twisting her fingers together. "Thank you. Amber was – she was so amazing," Megan said. "She was smart, funny, she had her whole life ahead of her. And she was only twenty-five."

She gave a sobbing sigh.

Katie nodded. "It's tragic. All I can say is we are working nonstop to find out who did this. It won't bring her back, but at least that will help you get closure."

"I guess that's all I can hope for," she said sadly.

"When was the last time you spoke to your sister?" Katie asked.

"I last saw her a few days before she died. And we spoke on the phone the day before."

"Did she mention being uneasy, scared, worried about anything? Had she noticed anyone following her, anything like that?"

"No. Nothing at all, and I'm sure she would have told me if there were any issues."

"Her work? I believe she's in the legal field. Any sensitive cases, any reason for concern there?"

"No. The law firm she worked for specialized in tax and company law. Nothing that could cause any trouble for anyone working there. She actually told me it was pretty boring."

"What about her personal life? Had she been dating anyone recently?"

"Amber was seeing someone. Name of Ian Ingram. She broke up with him a couple of months ago. He was a horrible man. And he did threaten her afterward. In fact, she got a restraining order against him."

Katie sat straighter. Finally, there was evidence coming to light that might just have a bearing on this case. An abusive ex was significant. It might even be the lead they needed.

"What exactly did he do when they broke up?"

"He sent her a lot of nasty emails, called her names, told her he was coming after her. He went to her work office once, but her bosses told him to leave, and promised that they'd call the police if he arrived there again."

"Did he keep harassing her?"

"Not after the restraining order. But right up until that time, yes. Calling her, texting her, driving past her house."

Katie glanced at Leblanc, who looked equally disturbed by this bombshell. And then she looked questioningly at Rix. She was certain that the police already knew about this troublesome ex. What had they found out?

Rix cleared his throat.

"We already interviewed Mr. Ingram. He had an alibi for that evening."

"What was his alibi?" Katie asked.

"He was at a bar with his friends. His new girlfriend confirmed that he'd been there from around eight o'clock."

Katie shook her head.

"I don't fully trust a version that's confirmed by a new girlfriend and by friends. They could easily be covering for him."

"You think they'd do such a thing?" Rix said dubiously. "Knowing the seriousness? We did confirm it by speaking to three different friends, individually. We unfortunately couldn't confirm with the bar staff as it was an extremely busy night."

Katie shrugged. "If he's a manipulative guy, he might have pre-warned all of them that he'd really been home alone but that the police would get him into trouble if he said so. Something like that. Making it easier for them to lie on his behalf."

"He was manipulative," Megan agreed.

"Do you know if he was ever in trouble with the law in other ways?" Katie turned her focus back to Megan.

"No. I never heard about anything like that. But I suppose it's possible."

"He has no criminal record," Rix said.

Katie nodded. "And his job?" If Ian was the killer, he would have needed to go to Vancouver to commit the second crime.

"He's a salesman for some computer firm," Megan said.

"Does he travel for work?"

"Yes," Megan said. "He was on the road for three weeks before Amber broke it off with him. And that was after a big sales meeting in New York."

"How well did you know him?" Leblanc asked.

"Not very well. I met him a couple of times. He seemed okay at first, but you could see he was a controlling person and I was sure he would be one of those jealous types. Then he became possessive, and it was obvious that he was obsessed with Amber."

"What was he like physically?" Katie asked.

"Tall, strong. He had short blonde hair, brown eyes. He was good-looking in a way, but there was something off about him. A hardness."

"Was he an aggressive person, do you think?" Katie probed.

"Yes. He was definitely someone who would want to fight. Not a gentle man," Megan said with a sigh. "He could easily get angry, and it was obvious that he had a short fuse."

"Was your sister afraid of him?" Katie asked the question carefully, and Megan considered it for a few moments before answering.

"I'm not sure. She never said so, but I think she might have been. At any rate, she made a very firm decision to call it off. I don't think I'd have liked to go through what Amber went through with him."

"How did he take it when she broke it off?" Leblanc asked.

"He was immediately furious. He hated that she'd made that decision. He went off the rails. I remember one of the threats she told me about, where he said it was only a matter of time before he'd have her."

"Did he talk about how he'd do it?" Leblanc asked.

"No." She gave a shiver. "That's what was frightening."

"There were no more incidents after the restraining order?" Katie asked.

"No. And I think Amber was relieved. But she kept being watchful. At first, anyway. But time goes by and when nothing happens, I guess people start feeling as if life is normal again."

"Do you know if Ian has a car?"

"Yes. He has a black Camaro."

That was another detail that might be helpful, Katie thought.

For now, she decided she'd gathered enough information and had a direction to pursue.

"I want to express our condolences once again," Katie said. "If you think of anything that might help us, please let us know."

"I will," Megan said. "And thank you. I just want to know who did this. My sister was happy, and then suddenly, she was dead. I still can't really believe it and don't know if I ever will. Nothing about this makes sense."

Katie thought the relationship with the ex was looking more and more suspicious, and she couldn't wait to investigate it in detail.

26

To her, a man with a temper, and a restraining order against him, was a very typical personality to have committed a violent crime against the woman who rejected him. It was time to find out if Ian Ingram had done exactly that.

CHAPTER SIX

An hour later, Katie and Leblanc pulled up outside the apartment block where Ian Ingram lived.

Since he was a salesperson and they had no idea where he would be at two-thirty in the afternoon, Rix had called him and asked him if he could come by his home to sign a statement. It was an innocent subterfuge to get him to a place where he could be questioned.

But Rix would not be at this meeting. Katie had decided she and Leblanc should go in alone to question him. She felt expectant about this interview, and knew she might need to be on her guard.

She walked up the stairs to the second-floor apartment. The seven-story building had a view of downtown Seattle, all concrete and streets and rooftops, interspersed by splashes of greenery and rows of trees and, at this time, whitened by snow.

Katie knew she'd have to bring all her skills to this interview, because she was up against someone who would most likely not hesitate to lie, and might already have done so.

She lifted her hand to knock at the door, but it opened before she could touch it. Ian Ingram stood in the doorway.

He was a big, blonde man, with broad shoulders and a barrel chest.

His face was clear and rather handsome, with a square jaw and a straight nose, but his eyes were cold and hard.

He seemed taken aback to see them.

"I was expecting Detective Rix," he said. "Are you part of his team?"

"Separate investigators, but on the same case," Katie explained. "Mr. Ingram, we need to confirm a few details from the night of the crime."

"Can we sit down?" Leblanc asked.

"Sure. Come in. The place is a bit of a mess. I haven't had time to clean up and had no idea you were coming."

Ian didn't sound too pleased as he led the way into the apartment, which was expensively furnished, but untidy. The leather lounge sofas were sumptuous, but dirty coffee cups and plates were scattered on the coffee table.

As they spoke, Katie took a quick look around the apartment. There was no sign of a current girlfriend, although the numbers of plates and cups signaled that company had been over last night.

"Is there really a need to question me again?" he asked irritably as they sat.

"Yes, there is," Katie said. "We have a few details that we need to clarify."

"This is all ridiculous," Ian said. "I didn't kill Amber. I know you'd love to pin the crime on me. But if you insist on dragging me through the mud, I'd at least like to know where I stand."

There was a note of menace in his voice that made Katie take heed.

"You're not being accused of anything," she said. "We're just asking you to verify the statements you've given us."

"I've given you everything," he said flatly. "I've already said that I didn't do anything wrong. I was genuinely horrified when I heard she was dead. I mean, I actually cried. It's shocking. She must have pissed someone off real bad, but that person was not me and I did not kill her. There was no need to get a restraining order, but I accepted it and complied with those terms!"

"Could you just check a few details for us?" Katie said quietly.

"I suppose," he said grudgingly. "Like what?"

"Did you threaten or assault Amber at any time?" Leblanc asked.

Ian's eyes narrowed in anger. "No. I never touched her."

"But she was afraid of you? Afraid enough to get the police involved?"

"I never touched her," he repeated, his voice rising to a shout.

"Are you sure?" Leblanc asked.

"Of course," Ian said, controlling his anger. "I may not be the best boyfriend in the world, but I never laid a finger on her. You can ask her friends. Or her sister. Or anyone else. She had a restraining order against me, but no one ever saw me do anything to hurt her."

"I see," Katie said. "Can you give us your account of your movements on the night of Amber's murder?"

"I told you before," he said. "Why do you need that again?"

"Mr. Ingram," Katie said patiently. "We are in the course of investigating a murder. We will check everything you've told us, but it's easier if you verify that information for us now."

"Fine." He sounded annoyed. "I got home about five-thirty. I was with a client all afternoon, discussing a purchase. Then I went out at about six-thirty to a bar. I met a few friends there, had some drinks, and got home around ten."

"Which bar?"

"The Caribbean Bar. It's about two miles from here."

Katie took the notebook out of her briefcase and made a note of that.

"I don't know why you need to know this," he said, sounding annoyed. "I told you I got home about ten. You're going through the details again for no reason."

"Yes, we are," Katie said. She didn't get defensive. She found his own defensiveness very interesting and it told her a lot about him. Now it was time to drill down further into his alibi.

"Can you tell us who you met at the bar?" she asked.

"I met a few friends there."

"Names of?" Leblanc pressured him.

"George, James, Steve, Tracy, and Kim, who's – er - a good friend."

He didn't mention she was his new girlfriend, Katie noted.

"Did anyone see you leave the Caribbean Bar, or get into a car? Can anyone confirm when you left?"

"Probably not," Ian said.

"Why not?" Leblanc asked.

"I don't know. I guess no one was watching the time that closely. I was in a group of people. The place was packed."

"Is there anyone who can confirm that you got home at ten?" Leblanc asked.

"Look, I don't see why you won't take my word for it," he blustered. "We were not watching the clock. Just socializing."

"Did you drive straight home?" Katie asked.

"Yes," Ian said, but he looked down at the floor.

"Where does your work take you?"

Ian sighed. "I go to Canada regularly. I travel east, as far as Ohio. My sales territory is the northern Seattle area, as far as northern Vancouver."

"Were you away recently?" Leblanc leaned forward, scrutinizing him closely.

"I got back this morning from a field trip to Vancouver yesterday."

Katie had to fight not to show her shock at this coincidence. If the police had interviewed him straight after the murder, not even they would know about this.

"Are you trying to trap me or what?" Now Ian sounded aggressive, as if they had him cornered. "I can show you my passport. I was there! Not here!"

That was interesting. So he thought being there would prove his innocence?

"When you were in Vancouver, what time did you get up this morning? What did you do?" Would he have been prowling around downtown early in the morning, or have had the opportunity to go there?

"I got up at seven, and had breakfast at the hotel."

"Which hotel?"

"The Marriott."

"Did you rent a car?"

"Yes. I can show you the papers."

Katie nodded.

There would undoubtedly be cameras at the Marriott, which could be used to confirm if he'd taken his rental vehicle off the premises early in the morning. Finally, they had a way of confirming Ian's whereabouts for one of the two murders.

"And then?" she asked.

"Then I went to the airport. Here, look."

Ian got up and dug clumsily in his briefcase, which was leaning against the coffee table.

As he did so, Katie realized the reason for his clumsiness.

His right hand seemed unable to fully close. Now that she was looking closely, she saw a jagged scar protruding from his shirt sleeve. Even his knuckles were scarred, as if he had been seriously burned and the skin had not healed correctly.

"What happened to your hand?" she asked.

"I was in a car crash a year ago. My arm got smashed up really bad. I've got permanent nerve damage. Had to stop a lot of the things I enjoyed," he said sourly. "Gym. Weightlifting. Tennis. I used to play league tennis. But I can't play well enough with my left."

Katie's mind was racing.

The coroner had indicated that from the angle, the blows were made by a right handed attacker.

But Ian couldn't close his dominant hand. It was damaged and weakened.

She didn't necessarily believe his alibi for the night of Amber's murder, and thought he'd asked his friends to cover for him because he didn't want trouble, but she could see that he would definitely not be able to inflict a killing blow with the axe using his right hand.

"Thank you," Katie said.

She would still request the footage from the hotel, but for now, it looked as if this line of investigation was nothing more than a frustrating dead end.

It was time for them to travel to Vancouver, in the hope that the circumstances surrounding the second murder victim, Melany Mason, would yield more evidence.

Melany had briefly seen the killer and Katie held out hope that she had described him or given some indication of what he looked like, but that in the trauma of discovering her body, Stephanie had forgotten about it. Memories sometimes worked that way, Katie knew.

Perhaps now, a few hours later, she might remember more that would give them a clue to his identity.

CHAPTER SEVEN

As Katie neared Vancouver, she saw that the drive north had taken them closer to three hours than the two and a half she'd expected. Already, she felt as if they were experiencing hitches and delays every way they turned in this case. The reason for the delay this time was that they'd headed into increasingly heavy weather. A mixture of rain and sleet was cascading onto the windshield of the car they'd borrowed from the Seattle police department.

Going into downtown, they saw streams of cars heading the other way, driving out for the afternoon rush. Their lights were bright against the deep gray clouds and driving rain that seemed intent on shutting the city's activity down.

They were heading straight to the second crime scene. Melany had been killed outside the bakery where she worked, and Stephanie, her co-worker, had agreed to come in again and be interviewed on site.

Katie thought that was very brave of her.

As they parked across the road, Katie could see a few people were sheltering under the overhang outside the bakery. News vans were parked across the street, with the reporters and camera crews hurrying, umbrellas bobbing, between the bakery and the police tape that still cordoned off the area.

Again, she thought how incongruous such a crime was, to have happened right under this bakery's cheerful pink and white signage.

There was a local RCMP officer monitoring the scene. Swathed in a yellow waterproof coat, he hurried over as soon as they approached. He looked to be in his mid-twenties, tall and lean, and seemed very disturbed by what had happened in his precinct.

"You'll be the cross-border task force?" he asked.

"Correct," Katie said.

"The body's been removed, of course. There was a downpour this morning that's back again now, as you can see, so searching for trace evidence was pretty much impossible, but here's where it happened."

He led them over to the chalk outline that was partially visible under the rain-spattered overhang.

Katie saw the dark traces of blood still visible on the paving. She shivered, and not just from the unfriendly wind.

"The coworker who found the body called us immediately. We were able to cordon off the scene and we set up a roadblock on the nearest main road, but it looks as if we acted too late, as we didn't pick up anyone or anything suspicious from it."

"Any possible camera evidence?"

"There's one traffic camera a couple of hundred yards away, on the main road. We're checking that footage, but with the amount of rain this morning, I'm not optimistic we'll get anything usable," the officer explained. "The killer could also have approached from a different direction, or arrived via the back roads. If someone had parked nearby, and walked here, they could have waited basically unobserved in this weather."

Katie nodded, guessing that the perfect camera shot was too much to hope for. Nothing about this case signaled that it was going to be easy.

"Do you have photos of the body?"

"Sure."

He led them into the bakery itself, where he set up a laptop.

Katie stared at the screen. In the rain, and with the victim's black clothing, they almost looked to be in grayscale, rather than color. Somber shades for a terrible scene. Zooming in, she saw that, again, the victim had been hit in the back of the head. Again, it looked to have been an extremely violent, powerful blow.

It would have killed Melany almost immediately, she guessed.

One thing that drew Katie's attention as she looked closer, was that Melany seemed very similar to Amber in terms of looks. She also had that thick, shoulder-length brunette hair. She, too, was slim, and seemed of average height.

"Do you think that's a coincidence?" she asked Leblanc in a low voice. "They're very similar looking. Is he seeking out a certain type?"

Leblanc frowned. "Yes. They could almost be sisters. Perhaps he is."

"But if so, why?" That was the question which Katie knew would get them further, but as yet they had no answers.

The killer, and his weapon, had disappeared into the rain-swept early darkness, leaving Melany's poor colleague to discover the scene.

She'd walked in about fifteen minutes later, according to the timeline that the RCMP officers had sketched out.

"Stephanie is waiting here," the officer said.

Katie moved to the bakery's side office, to greet the witness who had found the body and known Melany.

Stephanie was a small woman with a cloud of blonde hair, an oval face, big eyes, and an expressive mouth. Katie thought she would be a beauty in better circumstances, even though she looked devastated and forlorn at this time.

Katie gave her a sympathetic nod as she showed her badge.

"I'm sorry about the loss of your colleague, Stephanie. You've had an extremely traumatic day and we're grateful that you're here and able to speak to us. We'd like to ask you a few questions about her."

"Sure. I'll - I'll try."

Her voice was soft, and trembled as she spoke.

""What can you tell us about Melany?"

"I'd known her for a year. She moved back to Vancouver and got this job after her mother died. She'd been living in Toronto for a while, I think. She was really nice. Very hard-working. She enjoyed her job. She was always first into work."

"Did she have a boyfriend, any close family?"

"Not in Vancouver. She was actually sort-of dating someone she'd met in Toronto, and they used to get together every couple of months. She had no family here."

"Any trouble in her life, any clashes, anything strange or disturbing that she mentioned in recent weeks?"

Katie remembered from the sketchy briefing they'd had that there had been, and hoped she might now learn more.

"No trouble, but she did mention to me last night that she thought she'd been followed."

Hoping that Stephanie might remember more, Katie nodded.

"What did she tell you about that? Perhaps you might have remembered a few details?" Katie asked, hoping for any evidence to take them further.

"We were on a call yesterday evening, discussing the bakes and schedule for the morning, and she mentioned it as a sort of aside," Stephanie explained. "I'm trying to think of her exact words. She said that she felt someone was following her, and that when she tried to get a look at them, they had, like, disappeared. Run away. She said it was weird, and that she'd taken a different route home."

"Did she say she felt uneasy about coming into work today?"

Stephanie sighed.

"On our way home, it's mid-afternoon, and the whole of downtown is very busy. Coming to work it's always quiet and feels like a different world. I guess she never thought anyone would be waiting, at that hour."

But someone had been.

"Did you ask her anything else about it?"

Stephanie looked abashed. "I wish I had. But she was the one who got the conversation back on track for work." Then she raised her eyebrows. "You know, she did mention that Peter, her boyfriend in Toronto, would be calling her at eight. So she might have told him more about it. She used to tell him everything about what went on in her life."

"Do you know Peter's details?"

"Sure. I do. He used to call the bakery from time to time to speak to her. I can look up his number for you."

Stephanie moved over to the computer and took a look at the call records.

"Here you are. I don't know if this is his home or work number, but it's the one he used." She read it out.

"Does Peter know yet what's happened?" Katie asked.

Stephanie frowned. "I'm not sure about that. He might not know yet. I think the police were contacting her father - he was divorced from her mom, and lived in Calgary. But as far as I know, Melany wasn't close to her dad at all."

Katie nodded. Undoubtedly, their call to Peter would be a huge shock, but at least now she was prepared and knew what she would have to say.

"Thank you again for coming in," Katie said. "How are you getting home?"

Stephanie frowned, looking unsure.

"Let us drive you home," Leblanc offered.

From the gratitude on the baker's face, Katie saw that getting home had been something she'd dreaded. She was glad Leblanc had offered this help, to get her through what would otherwise have been a stressful

- and potentially even dangerous - ordeal, because who knew where this killer was hiding now?

"Do you think I'm in danger?" Stephanie asked, clearly thinking along the same lines herself.

Katie shook her head. "At this stage, I don't know. We haven't learned enough about this criminal yet. Please, be careful. Ask the police to wait for you, or walk with you, when the bakery reopens. At any rate, until he's caught."

"I will," she said somberly.

They walked briskly across the rainy street and climbed into the car.

Katie started it up, listening to Stephanie's directions as she navigated the short drive.

Inwardly, she was feeling frustrated, and more than a little anxious about their lack of progress. The fear that these murders created, the impact that this was already having on people's lives, was deeply troubling.

And yet, this killer was elusive. Nobody had seen him. A big, strong man with an axe had managed to murder two women in suburban or urban settings and had been able to melt into invisibility.

Katie hoped that Melany would have confided more in the boyfriend, and that Peter might hold information, or a description, that would get them a step further.

CHAPTER EIGHT

Fear. That was what the music man felt. He felt a chilling, bone-deep fear that seemed to sear all the way into his soul.

How was it possible that this woman had done what she did? He didn't believe in witchcraft, spirits, ghosts, demons, or the world of the unseen.

But with a sick sense of acceptance, he now understood that maybe, that world believed in him.

He had his axe. It would protect him. The axe had worked to destroy her, but he knew it didn't work to prevent her coming back.

He knew he needed to go back to the place he never wanted to visit again, but he would have to go there now. It was the only solution. He'd omitted a step and now had to complete the circle.

And while getting there, he'd have to keep to himself, away from the cities and towns. She'd never appeared to him in the woods - yet. She seemed to like more crowded places, where people congregated. That was fine, because the music man had never loved those kinds of places.

Now he'd have to head back to Vancouver Island and face his worst nightmare again.

What if she was there, waiting?

Fear clenched at him again as he considered the prospect. He felt sick inside. His hands felt wet. Instinctively, his right hand clenched, ready to raise his weapon.

If the worst happened, he had no idea what he would do, but at least he would have time to prepare and be ready for her.

Now, he had to hurry. He had to get away from her because, perhaps, his own slowness was allowing her to keep finding him again and again. He wondered if she was here, somewhere, watching him. Perhaps she was. He could feel her presence. He could feel her cold gaze.

He breathed out, shaking all over, feeling the sense of dread and the chilly sweat begin to overpower him again. The fear was cold and deep and numbing. It paralyzed him and froze up his logical thoughts, leaving him helpless to do anything but run, after trying to defend himself the only way he knew how.

With the decision made, he knew he had to act fast.

The music man packed his few possessions up in a small backpack, grabbed his axe and lifted his guitar case. He liked the feel of the axe, its weight and heft, the power and confidence it gave him.

He stroked the blade with his fingers and felt the cold chisel edge. It still felt as deadly and sharp as it had when it was new. It was a great weapon, and he had put it to good use.

Until the unthinkable time that still haunted him. The moment that had changed his life.

He said the words to himself like a mantra. "She will not find me again after I've done what I need to do. I will be safe there."

He thought that when he'd done what he had to, he would stay on the island. The thought of being away from the crowds and the cities, where he could live in the woods, where he could hunt and protect himself, gave him a sense of relief. Perhaps there could be an end to this fear, one day.

He crept out of the basement where he'd hidden for the whole day, and cowered away into the cool dark night. It was the early hours of the morning. Three, maybe four a.m. The city was quiet.

There was a slight mist, and the rain had stopped. The parking lot across the road was almost empty. It was still far too early for many to be up.

He stopped and turned around.

There was nobody there. He could see nobody who might be watching.

Nobody.

But then, a distant noise caught his ear, a car in the distance. But he knew it was no car. She had found him.

Terror was instant and overwhelming. He was aware of his heart pounding in his chest. He could feel his pulse in his ears.

So close. He could feel her near him. Her presence. She had found him after all. Now, he would die.

He had to hide.

Wait, he thought; but he could not wait. He ran, fast and strong, his heavy shoes pounding on the sidewalk as he took his first few steps. He wanted to scream, but he couldn't. He wanted to cry out for help, but he felt as if his throat and mouth were frozen.

He did not look back as he ran; he did not dare look back. He could sense her a couple of streets behind him. He twisted and turned through the city, running down the alleyways and side streets to keep from being seen. He took shortcuts, backtracked, even cut through a building and out the back way, trying to lose her. Even though he moved as fast as he could, he knew that she was right behind, gaining on him. He could feel the tug of her presence, the cold, dead hand at his back.

He had to get her before she got him.

Glancing over his shoulder, he thought he saw her eyes, her face. He had never seen such hatred, such malevolence. There was no humanity in her eyes.

This was no normal woman, no, no, no. It was the demon, the ghost, the spirit. That was who she was.

He ran faster, but it wasn't enough. She kept pace; she kept running after him. She could do the impossible and that was what made her so deadly. Because she was not alive, and she wanted to take his life.

This is it, he thought in despair, as he jogged down the street, gasping for breath. This is the end. He ran on and on, until exhaustion slowed him, and he dropped back to a walk.

Hesitantly, he turned and checked once more, and he saw that he had managed to outpace her at last. He couldn't see her eyes behind him any longer, or that blowing, shiny brown hair. For now, they were gone, and she had retreated.

All it had taken was every inch of his strength. He couldn't keep doing this. His legs were shaking; his lungs were burning.

He turned a corner and saw to his surprise that he had run all the way to the highway bridge. Ahead, were signs to the main road that led to the ferry, and to the place where he could find safety.

He had to get onto that island. He was on his own in this, he knew, and had never felt so alone. He had no friends, nowhere to run and no one who would help. He was entirely at her mercy.

But he couldn't use the main road. Too many people. He needed to detour, and get to the ferry via a quieter route.

He breathed heavily, trying to subdue his panic, and make a plan as he limped along, hoping that some strength would filter back into his aching legs.

He didn't have a car here. So he would need to get a ride. He could do it, he knew. The guitar case would help him, and there was something about his face that he had learned made that particular thing easy. Perhaps it was his even features, even though his hair and beard were somewhat overgrown. Perhaps it was his eyes, wide and a warm shade of hazel brown, or his wide chin. He had regular, strong features, and when he smiled, even his teeth were white and straight and clean.

His hands, though big, rough, and callused, were neatly kept. Once, that had been because of his music. Now, it was just because of habit. No more than that.

The music man limped down the streets, veering away from the main road, heading for the closest side street, looking to get out into the countryside where people would take the back roads to one of the ferry terminals. He didn't mind which one he got to.

He stuck out his thumb, hoping for a ride at this early hour, even though it would be a couple more hours yet until daylight.

He pasted a smile on his face and slung his guitar case over his shoulder, so people could see it, and believe he was a traveling musician.

Except that case no longer held any guitar. He'd never had much use for it, and had only kept it for the memories. It hadn't felt like a wrench to abandon it, but rather like a necessary step.

Now, the case was home to a heavy, sharp axe with a bloodied blade.

CHAPTER NINE

Leblanc hurried into the conference room behind Katie. They'd decided to use the closest hotel to make the urgent call to Peter, hoping that Melany might have shared some important details with her boyfriend.

The warm, carpeted room had a small table, six chairs, and an oak-paneled wall at the back.

As he entered the room, Katie cast him a sad look.

"I hate this," she murmured. "I hate it."

Suddenly, Leblanc felt a tug of emotion, in his heart and gut. He wanted to embrace her and to say everything would be fine, but he knew it wouldn't, and wasn't going to be. Not for a while longer. Not until this killer was caught.

"It's going to be okay soon," he said. It was all the reassurance he dared to give.

They sat down and set up their laptops and phones. Then Katie dialed Peter's number and put the phone on speaker when it rang. Leblanc felt a frisson of dread as he waited for the man to pick up.

"Hello?" a man's voice answered after the fourth ring. He sounded breathless, as if he'd rushed to grab the phone.

Leblanc saw Katie's face, hard and resolute.

"Is that Peter speaking?"

"Yes, that's me. Peter Kent," he said, sounding curious.

"It's Agent Winter here, from the FBI. I have some tragic news regarding Melany, your girlfriend in Vancouver. Do you need to do anything to be prepared before I tell you more? Would you like to go somewhere private, or ask anyone to be with you?"

"Regarding Melany? Melany?" He sounded incredulous. "I - I don't know what I need to do. What has happened?"

"It's not good, Peter. She has been murdered."

"What?" His voice rang out and Leblanc could not keep from flinching.

Katie kept her eyes on her computer screen, appearing calm, but Leblanc couldn't help looking at her hands. She was gripping the phone like it was a lifeline. Perhaps it felt that way to her.

"This can't be true! Is it a joke? What is this, a prank call?" His voice was high and hysterical.

"I'm so sorry. This is the hardest part of our job," Katie said.

It was the calm sureness of her voice that seemed to convince Peter. He let out a long, shuddering sigh.

"I - I still don't believe it. I need time to take it in. What happened?"

Leblanc knew Katie would gloss over the details. Now was not the time for this man to know the full horror of her death.

"She was attacked outside work, early this morning. It doesn't look like a robbery. It seems she was targeted but we don't know if she was in the wrong place at the wrong time, or if there was another reason," Katie said.

"I can't imagine anyone would want to kill her. Anyone. At all." Peter's voice shook.

Katie waited. Leblanc could see the tiny movements of her eyes as she assessed each note of his voice, each hitch of his breath. Because this was not just a courtesy call. They needed information from him.

And Katie was waiting to assess the right time to ask.

Now, Leblanc saw. Now she was going to steer the subject where she needed it to go.

"I understand from her colleague, that Melany thought she was being followed last night. It might be important to this case if we were able to know more. Do you know anything else about what happened last night? Did she tell you?" Katie asked gently.

Peter drew in another astounded breath.

"Oh, geez, yes, she did say that. She was being followed; she told me about it. And now she's dead. Can you find this man?" he asked in strained tones.

"Can you tell us what she said?"

"She made a funny story out of it. She said there was this guy, this big, strong guy with a short beard, who was looking at her weirdly when she crossed the street. And being her, she turned and glared back at him and she said he literally ran away!"

"Is that so?" Now Leblanc could see Katie was frowning.

"Yes. It was very strange, she said. We discussed it, and she told me she'd wondered if he was some kind of informer for a gang, and if he was running away to call some of his friends and get her mugged at a traffic light. So she changed direction and took a different route home."

"Did she mention anything else about him?" Katie asked as Leblanc hoped for more clarity.

"No. I wish I'd asked her more. But she didn't make a big thing out of it. Like I said, it was more a funny story than anything, but that was Mel for you. She wasn't a fearful person at all. She was very brave."

"Is there anything else she mentioned? Anything at all?" Katie asked, her voice encouraging.

"No. Nothing. I wish she had said something. Do you think I could have helped her somehow? Could she have said something that might have helped? Please - I need to know."

"I am absolutely sure there is nothing you could have done that would have changed this outcome in any way. And what you have told us has been helpful. If there's anything else you think of, please let me know. And we'll let you know if there's any news. You may reach me on my cell phone. It's open twenty-four hours."

"I will," he muttered."Thank you." His voice shook, he was crying now. "Thank you for calling me. I have to go now."

He disconnected the call.

Katie slumped in her chair, her face pale, her eyes closed.

Leblanc gave her a moment, and a few heartbeats later, she sighed, opened her eyes, and sat straighter.

"It seems there's something strange going on. That encounter Peter told us about was not what I expected to hear," Katie said. "The man ran away? Why would he do that?"

"It's odd. But it doesn't get us much further," Leblanc said reluctantly.

He checked his watch.

It was dark, raining, and now after seven p.m. On this unpleasant night the city had shut down. He didn't think they were going to make any further progress, and might as well get some rest.

"Why don't we keep working here for a while longer, and book in for the night. We should probably get some sleep, and have an early start tomorrow."

"I agree," Katie said.

Neither of them were willing to admit the hard truth that the killer could be anywhere by now, and might well be planning to kill again.

Although Leblanc wished he could be out, watching and waiting, he knew in a city of millions, it would be impossible to be in the right place at the right time. If the killer was even still in Vancouver. They had no proof of that, as they didn't know enough about his habits. But it was possible he'd fled somewhere else.

"I'll go and sort out the rooms."

As he stood up, a strange thought occurred to him and he wondered for a moment if he should ask Katie whether they should book one room, or two.

Then Leblanc caught himself.

What had he been thinking? He'd nearly embarrassed himself. He was practically blushing for having made such a bold assumption. They were work colleagues!

But for a moment, he'd suddenly wondered if they might be more. They'd felt close recently. Closer than two colleagues. But even so it would be wrong to ask.

Or would it? Maybe now was the right time to ask this question, and get a clearer picture of what Katie thought.

Leblanc sighed. He couldn't do it now. The moment had passed. Two rooms it was, and would be.

And they could then spend another couple of hours reviewing the evidence. After all, when the pieces were set out on the board, it might be easier to see what they had missed.

There was always the chance that Peter, or even Stephanie, might remember a crucial detail that would take them further.

Wishing he'd had the guts to ask Katie about sharing a room, Leblanc trudged downstairs feeling thoroughly conflicted on all fronts.

He was trying to convince himself time was on his side, even though he knew it wasn't, and that they were lagging dangerously far behind a short-interval serial killer, who might strike again at any time.

CHAPTER TEN

There had to be some evidence they could use to take this case further, Katie agonized, a forgotten cup of coffee by her side as she reviewed her notes in the hotel's boardroom.

She felt intensely frustrated by the fact that the recent victim had most likely seen, actually seen, the killer. If only Peter had asked Melany more about him. If only Melany had described him more clearly, or taken a picture of him before he'd fled.

It sounded as if the bakery staff worked long hours, and Katie was puzzled by the fact that Melany would have seen the man when she left in the mid-afternoon, and that he'd been there again in the very early morning. Was he a local to the downtown Vancouver area? That might be worth exploring.

She made a note on it. Of course, then it raised the question of how and why he'd traveled to Seattle.

So many 'ifs', but they were left with no clarity and no progress.

She'd been looking at this over and over, and nothing new had surfaced. No nuance, no information, no different take. The victims had nothing in common apart from their appearance.

Reading her notes now and looking at the case progression so far, Katie felt a slight tightening in her chest. There were so many blanks. How could you track down someone like the man Melany described, when she hadn't really described him at all?

This wasn't getting them anywhere.

Opposite her, she heard Leblanc sigh too, rubbing his temples as he scrolled back over his own notes.

Katie picked up the coffee cup, drained it, and set it down. She felt frustrated and burned out.

And it was nearly nine p.m. She had been looking at the same notes for hours. She couldn't see any further; she'd gone over and over the same information, and the same thoughts.

She stood up, feeling impatient.

Katie knew she wasn't giving up, but she was wondering if they had missed something obvious. It might be that there was nothing here to take them further, at least nothing in the evidence that had been collected so far. It was as if a huge wall was suddenly in front of them, and there was no way for them to see over or around it to what was on the other side.

The worry she knew Leblanc shared, was that this man was on a short interval and might kill again at any time. What had sparked his killing spree, she wondered. He hadn't killed in the past using the same modus operandi, to their knowledge, until now. And now, he'd committed two murders in two different cities, just a few days apart. There must have been a tipping point that had catapulted him into these violent acts, but what had it been?

Going into his thought processes would provide desperately needed clues, but she didn't really have enough information on him yet to take even that simple step. But yet, she had to try.

What had made him decide to kill?

She had the sense that if they knew that, they might be able to predict the next one.

With a sigh, Katie walked to the door. Nothing was going to be gained by sitting here and she needed to move after being huddled at her computer for two solid hours.

"I'm going to get some air," she said to Leblanc. "I'll be ten minutes."

Looking up from his own laptop, he nodded. "I'll organize us some food from room service," he said. "Let's have some dinner here when you get back."

"Good idea," Katie said, feeling more positive, and suddenly hungry. She looked forward to food when she got back, but for now, she wanted to walk to that scene again.

Katie wrapped her coat around her, and headed outside into the driving rain. The bakery was only a few blocks away. She'd mapped Melany's route to work from her recorded home address.

Perhaps following her route would give Katie some clarity. She headed out of the hotel and into the cold, rainy evening. Then, she walked at a brisk pace, her coat hood pulled up over her head. The rain was refreshing on her face.

She felt a tiny surge of hope as she strode. Perhaps there would be something she could pick up from a second look at the scene, some small nugget that would help them.

As she hurried along the pavement, Katie checked the side streets. There was the bakery ahead, the crime scene tape firmly strung across the door. This was the starting point where Melany would have walked home. She'd mapped the two possible routes she would have taken. But she'd seen the killer before starting her journey, when she'd left work, if Peter had heard her correctly. So where would he have been?

Standing in the rain, Katie took a look around, hoping to see somewhere nearby where he might have stood that had a security camera. But the only place she could see was across the road, a stark, concrete frontage of an office block, with the lobby far down the street.

At this time, on this rainy night, downtown was very quiet, but there were still lights on in one or two of the offices.

Katie walked back to the crime scene tape. This had to be the place that Melany had been standing when she'd noticed the man watching her.

Melany would have felt safe, leaving in mid-afternoon.

However, standing here gave her an insight.

It would have been very easy for him to have stayed out of sight and followed her home. But according to Melany's version, he'd run off, hastily. Almost as if he'd been scared.

When she'd first noticed that the two victims looked alike, Katie had wondered if he'd been deliberately hunting down women who fit a certain profile. But the brief information that Peter had provided hadn't pointed to a hunt. She might be wrong, but that wasn't what she was sensing, and now that she was here, it wasn't what she was concluding.

Now that she was here, on site and looking around, Katie saw how incongruous this was.

If he'd been watching, waiting, why wouldn't he have stuck around to follow her? Where had he walked? Why had he left?

Had he noticed a policeman, an RCMP officer, someone who'd scared him off?

But there were plenty of people on the street in the mid-afternoon, and there was no reason for him to have thought he'd be seen as suspicious. Besides, that wasn't what it had sounded like.

Leblanc's theory was that he had followed her, then something had spooked him and he'd run off. Maybe he had seen someone else he knew, and that had frightened him off.

Was he just a crazy, unconnected, psycho-killer?

That didn't feel right either.

But what else was there?

Katie couldn't figure it out. The only bizarre conclusion she was able to reach was that the killer was somehow psychologically triggered by Melany, and had been looking to hide.

Was he attacking from a standpoint of fear? That could give her a clue about his behavior. In fact, it was the only thing that made sense. All he'd needed to do was walk a block behind her, or even further back, and he'd still have been able to see her.

But instead, he'd fled in such an obvious way that she'd noticed. He'd gone away to hide and had returned at a different time to kill.

Why? Had he acted out of fear? And if so was he afraid of being caught, or was it more complex than that?

Katie was aware of a faint sense of excitement, but it was so slight, she knew it would be nothing more than wishful thinking. However, anything that would help her understand him better would help her predict his actions.

A fearful man. Scared of his targets.

If that was so, then the immediate conclusion she drew from that line of thought was that he was psychologically damaged, that he'd had some kind of a psychotic break.

Katie turned around and started walking back to the hotel, her mind turning over everything, trying to imagine and predict, to read the killer's state of mind.

If he was acting from a state of fear, that gave her an insight she hadn't had before and it told her a little more about him.

Katie headed back to the hotel feeling thoughtful.

She wondered if this killer had experienced something in his past, either long ago or recently, that had tipped him over into these actions.

In that case, he wouldn't be hunting his victims. He would be running from them, killing in what he presumed to be self defense. That meant he would be very dangerous in an urban environment and would feel threatened by it. That would be unpleasant, confusing, and scary for him. If her intuition was right, he would not be looking to stay around in the city, but would be seeking to escape that environment, and go somewhere quieter.

But even escaping would put others at risk, if he saw a sight that triggered him again.

CHAPTER ELEVEN

Lynne Hobbs cranked the heater up and turned the music loud. It was another half-hour's drive to catch the ferry that would take her across to Vancouver Island. On the ferry itself, she planned to open her laptop, do some work. Get things up to date for the meeting later that morning.

Not that she could get everything up to date, because she'd messed up so badly, creating a situation that had spiraled way out of control.

She knew that the meeting was going to be tough. Very tough. She'd be asked questions that she couldn't answer, because there were no answers.

She glanced at herself in the rear view mirror. Wide, deep blue eyes. Shiny brunette hair, cut in a long bob. Clear skin. She looked innocent. Wholesome. And she was, really.

Lynne actually had no clear idea herself how, at the age of twenty-nine, she'd ended up stealing a significant amount of money from the charity that she had been managing.

It hadn't really been stealing, though, she tried to clarify. It had been borrowing. She was just not able to pay back what she'd taken.

Lynne wasn't sure how it had gotten so bad. She'd been caught short one month last year, when an ex-boyfriend had been in a bad situation and she'd helped him out. You see? She was looking out for others! That hadn't even been for her. He'd promised to pay the money back and he hadn't. Instead he'd flown off to Florida and changed his cellphone number.

Lynne had felt terrible, but she'd known there would be time to pay it back before the annual audit was done. But then things had gotten tough on her side. She'd had to stop sharing a place with a friend, and been forced to rent one of her own. She'd needed to move closer to work, and then she'd had to buy a new car, a good one, because her old jalopy had been on its last legs. And with the charity getting busier, she'd had to invest in some outfits, because her work took her to a lot of fundraisers and the pay wasn't great.

The day before the audit last year, she'd been full of fear, convinced she'd be in terrible trouble. Lynne remembered how sick she'd felt and how she'd woken up in the night sweating, and with her heart pounding, convinced that the next stop would be jail.

But in the end, it hadn't been that bad, because she'd gone back into the accounts and created some fake expenses that looked real and what she'd done had passed the basic scrutiny of the volunteer who'd completed the job.

The audit had revealed a small shortfall, but she'd been able to explain it away. She'd managed to put the blame onto an assistant who had left a few months previously and who had been careless with expenses. And they'd accepted that.

Like most of the people she knew, Lynne had been living paycheck to paycheck. But then, a month after the audit, she'd had the opportunity for a two-week vacation in Ireland. A place she'd always longed to go and knew she wouldn't be able to afford.

She had done it again. Skimmed off a couple of thousand dollars, and had the most incredible vacation. Memories that would last a lifetime. And she knew that the money she was taking would be easily camouflaged by the donations and transactions that would come flooding in during the next big drive. And of course, she would pay it back.

Everything had been a bit of a blur after that.

Lynne had tried to stop, but there was always some reason that it wasn't the right time. She'd been using the money to pay for a few luxuries, but also to help out a couple of friends who were in a bad situation. She hadn't only done it for her.

It hadn't seemed like stealing when you were doing it for someone else. And soon, it had spiraled out of control.

It became something she did without even thinking about it. And she'd lost the ability to stop.

A year later, and it was almost time for the next audit. But the problem was, the bookkeeper had been picking up discrepancies. She hadn't told Lynne, but had gone straight to the charity's board of directors.

This time they were doing a forensic audit, and Lynne knew her day of reckoning had come.

With a feeling of dread so powerful it made her nauseous, she acknowledged she was trapped. She'd been taking money out of the charity for so long that there was no way she could pay it back.

Her theft ran close to a hundred thousand dollars. In the space of a year and a half. She'd run out of room to create fake expenses. She'd been too scared to ask for a raise.

Lynne had a few credit cards, but despite the money she'd stolen, or rather borrowed, they were all maxed out. There was no way that she could afford to pay back her debt. And there was no way they wouldn't find her out.

That was the sort of thing a criminal did. The kind of thing you heard about on TV and shook your head disapprovingly, asking: but who would do that? What kind of monster would steal from a charity set up to help the elderly? Her parents would be devastated. Her brother, who was a sanctimonious little hypocrite at the best of times, would probably be all over social media about it, and then the whole world would know what she'd done.

She sighed. She was a good person. She really was.

Lynne returned to the present and turned up the music. She had no idea what she was doing now. She had no idea what to do about anything.

Another wave of nausea clenched her stomach as she turned onto the main road. Out of the corner of her eye, she noticed a man hitchhiking. Her lights flashed over him and for a moment she saw him clearly.

He looked tall, strong, ragged and ungroomed, but with a pleasant and likable face. An honest face. He had a guitar case slung over his back.

As she drove past, Lynne found herself hoping the guy would get a ride before the rain, which had eased to drizzle, came down hard again. And then the thought suddenly came to her. She should stop and help him out. She should give him a ride. Of course she should.

Immediately as she had the thought, misgivings crowded in. She was a woman alone, it was after dark, she had no idea who this man was.

But once she'd had the idea, her own guilt wouldn't let it go.

She might have stolen a substantial amount from the charity, but she was still a good person, the kind of person who would help a stranger. An open, trusting person.

Giving this guy a ride would prove she wasn't the criminal that everyone would soon think she was.

Before she knew what she was doing, Lynne slammed on the brakes and put the car in reverse. The lights illuminated his face, hopeful and relieved as he jogged toward her.

There. Her good deed for the day would be done and who knew how this might change the course of her life?

One act of kindness could change the world, right? And she sure needed her world changed right now.

She buzzed down the passenger window of her stylish, low-slung, brand new Mustang, bought last year courtesy of the charity, and leaned over.

"Are you headed to the ferry?" she called out.

He leaned in and stared at her.

And then his face changed. His eyes widened.

He looked as if he'd seen a ghost and for one absolutely terrible moment, Lynne feared that the word was out there already and that her photo was already in the news somewhere. That was her instinctive, gut reaction.

Then common sense prevailed. Of course it couldn't be so. But this guy looked terrified.

"I - I don't need a ride. Go! Just go!"

Lynne felt totally confused. This was her chance to prove her credentials, to square things up with her own conscience, and it was going terribly wrong. What was with this guy?

"Please, go! Leave me alone!" he entreated her, waving her on with a thick-fingered hand.

Normally, Lynne would have taken his advice. But for now, she felt wedded to the cause of helping him. Perhaps he needed help, she realized. She could call someone. Maybe he had family who could come and get him, or failing that, perhaps the cops. At any rate, someone who could get him off the road, where he was a possible danger in this state, and into the warmth.

She needed to do a good deed. She was going to do one, whatever it took.

"It's okay."

She put on her emergency lights and climbed out, holding her phone. The road was very quiet tonight. No other cars in sight. No other chance for this poor guy to get a helping hand.

"What's your name?" she asked. "Do you have family I can call?"

"No! No!" He backed away from her and she saw real panic in his eyes.

"Okay, okay," she soothed.

Now she felt absolutely hell-bent on helping him. She needed this karmic point. In her own mind, she was desperate to know that she'd gone out of her way to do good for someone before this damned meeting exploded in her face in a few more hours.

She opened her phone, ready to call the cops, but as she looked down, she saw there was a message from the charity.

Feeling that sick fear bubble in her again, Lynne quickly opened it.

She read a few of the words, before realizing that it was simply a confirmation of the meeting. But the tone was... austere. Not friendly. Accusing, even. They knew what she'd done and ice flooded her veins.

Glancing up from the message that had momentarily distracted her, Lynne prepared to continue with her good deed.

But the guy had gone. He'd disappeared.

That was simply weird. This was kind of impossible. Confused, she peered around into the darkness.

And then, from behind her, she heard a tiny sound.

She started to turn.

From the corner of her eye, she thought she saw him rush her, holding something that gleamed dully in the gloom.

What was it?

She needed to turn around to see. She needed to scream.

But Lynne didn't get a chance to do any of those things. With a massive, head-splitting bang, her world exploded in a burst of light, and then fizzled into a darkness that was absolute.

CHAPTER TWELVE

Katie was back in the prison cell again, facing Charles Everton. It was freezing cold. The cell was semi-dark and there was nobody else around. Just him and her, and she felt, with a clench of her stomach, he had the advantage here.

He stared at her, an unreadable expression on his angular face, and an evil light in his eyes.

"Do you want to know my secret?" he whispered.

"What is it?" Katie asked, feeling desperate. "Tell me."

"Oh, I will tell you. But first, you have to understand this."

"Understand what?" Katie felt that familiar dread.

"That I can do anything I want with you!" he hissed.

Then Everton began to laugh. A low, evil chuckle, laced with madness. It was a mirthless, chilling, crazy sound that grew louder and louder with every passing second.

Katie turned away, pressing her hands to her ears, trying to block it out, but it was in her head and it just wouldn't go away.

"No! Please, stop it! Stop it!" she screamed.

"Understand that you're the prisoner! I'm the one who's free. And this time, I'm hunting you," he taunted.

"No! No! No!" Katie screamed, pleading with him.

"I'll make you beg for my mercy, just like your sister did! You think we're in the prison? Of course not! We're by the river. You and me. It's a date. Are you ready?

Katie looked up and saw to her horror that there were no bars separating them now. They stood on the slippery bank, with dark, turbulent water rushing past. Storm clouds, boiling with energy and movement, raced across the sky and blotted out the moon.

"I'm coming for you, Katie," Everton shouted. "I've hunted you before, but this time I'm going to finish you! I'm going to kill you and laugh at your pathetic attempts to escape from me."

"No!" Katie screamed, but the words were ripped away from her by the wind, and lightning struck the earth, splitting the ground in front of her.

She threw her arms over her head and wailed in terror.

"No! Go away! Leave me alone!"

But Everton's laughter grew louder, and still his voice resonated in her head, his tone harsh and deep.

"See how easily I can make you scream? See how easily I can make you cry? Look how I can bring you to your knees?"

And just as she felt that she could endure no more, that she couldn't stand to be trapped like this in her own head any longer, he uttered one last threat in a low, growling voice.

"See how easily I can make you fall?"

His hands reached for her, and she was tumbling back into the icy, raging water, helpless and alone.

And then Katie's eyes flew open and she was instantly awake, panting and disoriented in the dark. She was shaking all over. Her temples were damp with sweat. The room felt claustrophobic, airless. Her heart was thundering in her chest.

Slowly, she got to grips with the terror that her nightmare had unleashed, but there was no way she was going back to sleep.

Before Katie could think too hard about what she was doing, she got out of bed and put on her hotel bathrobe.

Perhaps Leblanc was awake. She needed company, to be with him for a while. With her nightmare still looming in her mind, she wasn't going to think too hard about this decision.

She got up, opened her door, and padded across the carpeted corridor to tap on his room opposite.

Only then did she realize the enormity of her actions, of what she was doing. He would open the door to her, but she knew it might not be just a door he would be opening. Was she ready for this?

After a few seconds that seemed to last an eternity, the door opened a crack and his face appeared, eyes reddened with tiredness, but his eyebrows quirked in surprise.

"Katie? What is it?" he asked, a note of concern in his voice.

She took a step toward him. "Is it okay if I come in?"

"Yes. Yes, of course," he whispered.

She stepped into the room and he shut the door behind her.

"I had such a bad dream. I just needed your company for a while," she whispered. "Are you okay with it?"

"Of course," he replied. "Come in."

She stepped into the room. He closed the door. The heavy, dark wood felt like a barrier between them and the rest of the world.

The room was lit only by the faint light from the bathroom, and he stood in the shadows.

Katie felt as if she'd gotten this far and she had no idea what to do next. He couldn't exactly make coffee for her, or turn on the light. It was late, probably two a.m., and she'd dragged him out of a deep sleep. They both needed to rest.

"I – I don't want you to misunderstand," she stammered, now feeling totally thrown by her own actions.

"Come here," Leblanc said gently. "We both need to get some sleep."

Did she see the faintest of smiles on his face as he put his arm gently on her back and guided her over to the bed?

He climbed back under the covers. Going around the other side, she pulled back the duvet and got in. He drew her into his arms and held her, stroking her back and soothing her.

They lay like that for a few moments, and she felt her muscles relaxing, and the tension draining out of her.

This wouldn't be more, and she felt a deep relief knowing that. Neither of them wanted more, not now. This was enough. The comfort of his arms, his presence, was immense.

As she relaxed, her mind drifted and her thoughts became hazy. Katie took a deep breath and let herself sink further into that place where she felt safe and calm.

Then, she slipped back into sleep and this time, it was deep and dreamless.

*

She didn't know how much later it was that the persistent ringing of a phone yanked her from sleep. It was trilling loudly on the bedside table.

Not her phone. Hers was in her own room.

Leblanc's phone was ringing, and even as Katie struggled blearily to wakefulness, Leblanc stretched out his hand and took the call. He switched on the light. Sat up in bed. Checked the screen.

"Morning, Scott," he said, and Katie felt adrenaline jolt through her at their boss's name.

Immediately she saw his face change. She watched him listen intently, his brows knitting and his eyes narrowing.

"We're on our way. Send the coordinates," he said.

Katie sat up in bed, pushing her hair out of her eyes as Leblanc's phone beeped again with the incoming message.

"There's another crime scene," he told her, his tone brief and regretful. "A woman has been killed with an axe on one of the side roads south of the city, about ten miles from the Vancouver Island ferry."

Katie scrambled out of bed.

"What's the time?" she asked, needing to orient herself.

"It's six-thirty a.m.," Leblanc replied.

She was surprised she'd slept so well and deeply. But while she had been resting, this killer had been on the rampage.

"I'll be ready in ten minutes," she said.

Her thoughts already on the day ahead, she rushed back to her own room. She grabbed her clothes and dressed quickly.

She pulled her hair back into its ponytail, brushed her teeth, and splashed water on her face. Then she was ready.

As she left the room, her mind was racing with the implications of this new murder. Why had he done it? Why had he killed again, and was this woman going to be similar looking to the others? If only they had been able to stop him, but they just hadn't had enough information. The scarcity of evidence had worked in his favor, and now someone else had died.

She felt angry and frustrated that he'd killed again so fast. But perhaps his own speed was working against him. With speed came errors, and she hoped that this crime scene would provide new evidence to his identity, or even some clues about where he was headed.

CHAPTER THIRTEEN

Katie arrived at the crime scene just as a sullen dawn was beginning to brighten the sky. Yesterday's heavy rain was clearing, and the clouds were tinged with deep crimson.

She glanced at Leblanc as she saw the flashing lights ahead. For the first time, the scene was relatively fresh, and this would hopefully provide a better source of evidence. They'd traveled here in silence. She'd been strangely comforted by the memory of the past hours she'd spent in his arms, and wondered if he felt the same way.

But even so, she felt guilty that another woman had died. She felt personally responsible for not having done enough. Why hadn't she been able to predict his movements? Why had he killed here, on this road?

She stopped the car behind the emergency services vehicles. A RMCP officer in a reflective vest was waving other traffic away from the scene and detouring the cars onto a side road. Katie showed her badge and he waved them through. She parked a little further on, and climbed out.

Katie and Leblanc walked over to the scene and an officer hurried up.

"Winter and Leblanc from the special task force," she said.

"I'm Officer Bryce, the scene commander here. We haven't had the chance to do more than the basics yet. It was reported about half an hour ago. The forensic team has only just arrived."

"Who's the victim?" Katie asked.

"Ms. Lynne Hobbs, according to her ID and car registration. She must have been on her way to catch the earliest ferry. That's where this road goes. It joins the main road a few miles further on, and then goes to the harbor. From what we can make out, she pulled over and was attacked."

Katie looked at the sleek, new, silver Mustang. It was stopped by the side of the road.

"Could it have been a trap, an attempted carjacking?" she asked, and his brow furrowed.

"The strange thing is there's no evidence that this killer tried to take the car at all. If you put on foot covers and head covers, you're welcome to view the scene. Honestly, as far as I can make out, it seems as if she stopped, got out of her car for some reason, and then was killed. It doesn't tell a clear story and I'd appreciate your ideas on what happened here."

What had played out, Katie wondered, approaching the car. The body was sprawled below the car's open door, and the opposite window was open.

So she'd pulled over and then buzzed the window down. It seemed as if she had done that to speak to someone by the side of the road.

A hitchhiker, perhaps?

Then, for some reason, she'd climbed out of the car. That was what it looked like. And she'd been attacked from behind.

The blow was deep and brutal, perfectly accurate, bisecting her skull, and Katie saw it would have killed almost instantly.

Something glinted below her hand.

A phone? She'd gotten out to use her phone?

She saw Leblanc had noticed the same thing.

"Could she have been checking her phone? Did he ask her for information, directions, something like that?" he puzzled.

"Or pretended to be injured?" Katie theorized.

"Why would she have turned her back on someone with an axe?" Leblanc then asked.

"He's hiding it. He must be hiding it away. In a bag, or something like that. And then, he got her distracted and he attacked her."

She shook her head. There was so much about this scene that felt wrong and unknown.

But one thing she did now see, clearly, was that this was the same physical type of victim as the other two had been.

Though soaked with blood, her hair was thick, shoulder length, and brunette. She looked to be of average height and slim.

Katie felt a deep pity for her having lost her life, and frustrated that the circumstances were so confusing that it wasn't allowing her to piece together what had happened.

"It's the same guy," she announced. "That we can say."

"Yeah, I think we can assume so," Leblanc nodded.

"What about the car?" Katie asked, glancing at the Mustang. "Have you gone over it for any evidence, Bryce? Anything inside that might give us a clue about this guy?"

"Forensics are on it now. They've got it covered. But there seems to be nothing inside the car at all. It doesn't seem as if he was ever in there. That door is still locked."

Frowning, Katie looked inside the car and saw no sign of a fight. It was pristine, with not a trace of mud or blood. She breathed in the smell of new leather. An expensive looking jacket lay on the back seat.

No sign of a wet, muddy-footed hitchhiker inside the car.

Unfortunately, no sign of him outside the car either. If there had been footprints in the mud beyond the sidewalk, those would have been obscured by the softly falling rain that was now abating.

"She stopped to offer him a ride. But for some reason, he got spooked or fearful," Katie said, thinking back on what she knew from the other victim's account.

"So the number one question is, why did he kill her? She wasn't a threat to him," Leblanc said.

"Perhaps she asked him a question. Asked him where he was going. Or something else he didn't like."

Leblanc turned on his heel and paced thoughtfully away for a few steps, then turned back to face her.

"Maybe she got scared when she saw him up close and realized he was a big, strong guy."

Katie narrowed her eyes. "It might also have been the other way round," she suggested.

"What do you mean?" Leblanc asked.

"Perhaps her appearance spooked him. After all, if he was hitchhiking, he wouldn't have seen who stopped until they wound the window down."

Leblanc raised his eyebrows. "That's good thinking," he said admiringly. "Of course. There's no way he could have known who she would be."

"So there was something about this appearance, this type of woman, that triggered him. He began behaving strangely, who knows what played out, and it ended in him killing her."

Now the scene was starting to solidify in Katie's mind and she had more clarity. It was time to think forward. They'd pieced together as much as they could for now. The next question was: where had he gone? He hadn't taken the car. It seemed he hadn't wanted the car at all. He'd wanted a ride and then things had gone wrong.

She looked at the scene as a whole, taking it all in. There was a long stretch of road, surrounded by dense forest on both sides.

"He surely couldn't have hitchhiked again. Not after this, on such a quiet road. He must have fled the scene," she theorized. "Which means, if he was on foot, he's still in the area. And we know a bit about him. We know he's tall, has a short beard, and is carrying an axe with him that is concealed somehow."

These were all important facts.

"He was probably headed for the ferry. Perhaps he's still trying to get there, walking through the woods, taking a shortcut. Or he could have changed his plans about getting to the ferry, which means he's still here somewhere. In this area. Hiding out. Trying to regroup."

She felt as if she was gaining just a little traction on a slippery and dangerous slope. Not enough to catch up, but enough to dig in and prepare for the attack.

"Let's find this guy," she said with determination.

Leblanc glanced at her. In his eyes, she saw the same resolve burning.

"Let's do it," he confirmed.

"We're catching up with him. We're closing in on him, I feel sure," she added. "He doesn't seem to be driving a car, and he'd have a hard time stealing one now, with the roadblocks and patrols and police presence in the area. He's going to have to get where he wants to go on foot. I personally feel he'll stick to the minor roads and the tracks. Or possibly look for a shortcut through the forest, if he wants to hunker down for a while."

She stared around at the dense, dark forest. It was green and thick and it was hard to see more than twenty yards into it at any point.

That scenario was the best she could do, but she thought it covered all eventualities.

Leblanc gave her a quick nod and they both turned and walked towards the other officers.

Katie knew the killer was running. Alone, probably scared, and in the area. And they were in a position where at last, they could start the chase.

CHAPTER FOURTEEN

Leblanc sat in the car, having an emergency discussion with Katie. Time was of the essence now. They had identified a situation where the killer was almost certainly close by. But there was more than one way that they might find him and he wanted to propose a different tactic.

"We can organize a search, directly from here. Using as much manpower as can be made available," Katie said.

He could see she was focused on this option, wanting to get onto the road and physically track this man.

"How long will it take to organize it?" he asked, looking out of the window at the encroaching forest.

"We could start within minutes. I'm sure there could be backup here in less than half an hour. But we have to get everybody moving right now, to avoid losing time," she said, her voice firm and her expression determined.

He heard the excitement in her voice and understood it completely. This was her first real chance to get involved in the action on a level in which she was able to do something physical.

"It's important to get that going. But it will take a while to get organized. There's a wide area to cover."

Katie paused, staring at him ruefully. "True. It is a big area, and there are a lot of paths and tracks and minor roads crisscrossing it. And we've got less than an hour, most likely, until he's able to slip through," she said.

"Unless he's already slipped through," Leblanc argued.

"If he's going to the ferry, they'll be waiting for him. Everyone going on the ferry, and also coming off the other side of the ferry, is undergoing a full security search. Bryce has assigned two RCMP officers there to look for people who fit his basic description. He's instructed them that all tall, bearded men must be questioned about where they came from and provide ID and address details. There's no way that, even if he managed to get on there, he's getting off the other side without being fully checked."

"Agreed," Leblanc said.

"So we have a chance to find him here."

"What if he heads back into town? Loses us in the crowds?" Leblanc argued.

"I took a walk to the scene last night and tried to get a handle on his thinking. I don't think he'll choose to do that," Katie explained.

"Why's that?" Leblanc asked.

"I think he's running scared. Something in his environment, and possibly even the appearance of his victims, is triggering an aggressive fear reaction, or at any rate a desire to kill. But he's not leaving signatures. He's not proud of what he is doing, and doesn't even seem to be preplanning coherently. He's fleeing the scenes. He's looking, to me, like someone who wants to escape his predicament, to run away."

"So that means he's heading out of town?"

"Yes. That's what I think. It looks like he was aiming to get to Vancouver Island, but since he's making decisions on the fly, he might try another hiding place for now."

"You think that's his plan? It's not exactly sustainable," Leblanc argued, knowing that time was ticking by and that he saw nothing but resolve in Katie's green eyes.

The day was brightening and they had to make a decision fast.

"I think it's a temporary plan. I don't know whether this guy's thinking too far ahead right now. He's likely headed for somewhere where he thinks he can be safe for a while. He's on foot, and he's trying to get to a remote area."

"I guess you're right," Leblanc agreed.

"We're dealing with a very basic mindset here," she said. "He's in survival mode, I would say. He's psyched up and triggered and he's running. Look at the victims. He's not trying to be discreet or to hide them or anything."

"That's correct," he said. "So you go ahead and do that. We need to get the search going as soon as we can."

She was looking at him quizzically now.

"You want to try something else?" she asked. "What's your plan? Let me in on it."

"I think we should try a different angle."

She was silent for a moment. The only sound was the crackle of police radios from a few yards away, and the swish of traffic as it diverted onto the side road.

"What would that be?" she asked curiously.

"We haven't examined criminal records yet," Leblanc said. "We need to look for men who match up with crimes involving an axe. Men who match up with crimes involving younger women in this age group. He has now killed twice in Vancouver and it's likely that he's either a resident here, or he is spending a lot of time here. You know how often serial killers have past records."

Katie frowned.

"You don't think that can wait? This is urgent, Leblanc," she argued.

"It's a one person job. You'll only be one person short on the search," he countered.

"But you're a very important person."

He could see the stubborn set to her chin, and continued. "I'm not suggesting we don't do a physical search. I just think it would be a good idea to look for possible suspects as well. We can at least rule out some people who have a record."

He tried to pour as much reassurance into his voice as he could. She was silent, her expression unconvinced.

But he wasn't going to give up so easily on his line of thought.

"Every angle is important right now," he insisted. "Yes, the physical search is critical. But so is looking at past suspects. We could easily learn something that could lead us in the right direction. We could explore the situation intelligently."

He saw her face darken and hastily added, "Not that a search is not intelligent. Of course it is. I just meant that we can apply intelligence in two areas instead of one."

Suddenly, there felt like a lot of tension between them in the car. It hadn't felt that way two hours ago, when they'd been dozing in each other's arms. Even though they'd done nothing more than sleep, Leblanc still vividly remembered the feel of her skin. The smell of her hair. The way his heart had quickened when he'd heard that knock on his door.

Now, her eyes were glaring at him with green fire.

He could see that Katie was going to need a damned good reason for him to peel off on his own.

"Katie, I can connect the dots better than anyone. I'm the best analyst on the team and right now, you have a profile of a man clearly on the run. It's highly likely he's been in trouble before. We can do both of those things now because we have additional manpower. We won't always have the time or resources to explore two options simultaneously. You could even come with me and leave the police to search."

Now he saw fire in her eyes. She was angry because she thought he was trying to protect her.

And truthfully he was. He'd rather she helped with the research. A physical search for this killer was dangerous. Coming across a cornered criminal meant a high risk of attack.

"Are you trying to hold me back from doing my job?" she spat.

He shook his head. "Just looking to use resources where we can make the most progress."

He was amazed by his own calmness. Even so, he thought she was going to argue some more. He was readying himself for a fight.

But then, suddenly, she sighed.

"You're right. We do need to do that research," she admitted. "I would prefer it to be later, but as you say, we have the backup and manpower now. But I'm not coming with you. I'm spearheading this search."

There was going to be no derailing her and it was pointless to try, he acknowledged.

"I'll go to the main Vancouver police department right now and start processing through the records," Leblanc said.

"And I will organize the teams to search the forest, and start patrolling the perimeter roads going as far as the harbor," she said.

"There's a lot to do and little time to do it in," Leblanc said. "Let's get out there now."

"I'll get onto my side right away," she said.

"I will, too. Let's stay in touch. I hope that one of these angles gets us where we need to be."

As Katie got out of the car and strode over to the waiting police, Leblanc had the distinct impression that she thought his approach had better be good.

He sincerely hoped that his research angle would lead them the next step of the way.

And he hoped Katie would be safe.

It suddenly occurred to Leblanc, with a clench of his stomach, that she was very similar in age, appearance and build, to the three victims the killer had claimed so far. Out there, on her own, she might represent another target to him. Feeling anxious about her, he resolved to call and check up on her as soon as he could.

CHAPTER FIFTEEN

Katie climbed into the police car loaned to her by Officer Bryce, her mind focused on the search ahead. She was sure that the killer was hiding in these woods. It made all the logical sense in the world.

Briefly, she saw taillights flash as Leblanc headed off to do his part of their multi-pronged investigation. She hoped that he would also have a productive time, even though she'd resisted it at first, feeling that the search was more important. But she acknowledged that his research might uncover the identity of the very person hiding in these woods, and that would be helpful, especially if the search missed him.

The police car was a Ford Interceptor, a vehicle designed for speed. The engine hummed powerfully, and Katie gripped the wheel as she accelerated along the winding road that skirted the forest.

The area was in the process of being fully secured. The police were busy closing off all roads within a five-mile radius, and were bringing in more resources to patrol the perimeter. That meant that she and the other searchers would be able to start on the outside of the area and search every road and track that ran through this wooded area.

Of course, Katie knew there was a slim chance the killer had doubled back and escaped, caught a ride in the opposite direction, made a run for the quickest route elsewhere. But at this point she believed time was on their side, and he was still here.

The car radio crackled loudly, with constant streams of incoming messages and updates from the four separate vehicles, soon to be six, that were participating in the search.

"Any guidelines for search protocol?" the driver of the vehicle setting out to the west asked.

Katie thought quickly.

"I think we should concentrate our search in the area closest to the roadway, because if he's fleeing, that's where he is most likely to come out. So we focus on the perimeter first, then start moving inward."

"Copy that," the officer agreed.

"Officer Bryce, is there any chance of a drone flyover?" Katie asked.

Obtaining this would be a massive advantage, as it would be equipped with a heat sensor and would be able to look deep into the forest in a way that the searchers on foot couldn't.

"We have a drone, but it's currently in use," Bryce explained. "It's being utilized in a search for a missing person in the wilderness north of Vancouver. So it all depends if that person is located in time."

Katie nodded. She wasn't going to get her hopes up about the drone in that case. They would have to make do with what they had.

She drove on, slowing down to a crawl every time the foliage thinned or she reached one of the paths leading out of the forest. She gazed into the greenery, hoping to pick up a flicker of movement, or see someone hiding there.

"I've located an individual walking out of the woods," the other officer said and she felt a flare of excitement. "Male, on his own, looks to be in his late twenties. I'm going to stop him and question him."

"Be very careful," Katie warned.

"I am. I've got my partner close by. We'll be able to cover each other. I'll contact you if he looks to be suspicious."

She knew that there were likely to be a few innocent hikers in the woods, even at this early hour. It would be better to continue on her way, she decided, rather than rushing over there to provide backup. They needed to remain spread out and vigilant if this search was going to be a success.

"I'm going to continue on my course," she told the others.

"Copy that," Bryce confirmed.

Katie continued inching on. At this point, the forest was thick and wild with the undergrowth encroaching almost all the way to the road. It was a scenario that favored him, not her. It would be far too easy for him to hide away from a car.

The radio crackled again.

"That man has been cleared. He's a hiker who had a vehicle parked up on the south side of the woods," the officer reported. "He has evidence on his phone confirming that he was home with his two sons this morning."

"All good," Katie said.

At that moment, her phone buzzed in her pocket. She recognized Leblanc's number.

"Where are you?" she asked. "Is everything okay on your side?"

"I just got to the Vancouver police department, and they're accessing the records now. They're going to make everything available to me, going back the past four or five years. I'm waiting for the systems to run the search," he said. "But I was actually calling to make sure you were okay and to warn you to be careful. I was thinking as I left, that this guy has been targeting women who look a bit like you. In terms of hair color, height and so on. So you could trigger whatever it is that is driving him to kill."

Katie's eyes widened.

"I guess he is. The victims are similar to me," she agreed. "Thanks for the warning. I'll be very careful. I'm still patrolling the perimeter, looking for any signs. Hopefully we'll get lucky."

And then something caught her eye.

It was nothing more than a flash of pale among the dark leaves, but a moment later her mind realized what her eyes had instantly seen.

That it looked like a face. Like someone who hadn't wanted to be seen. It had been an oval, with a dark, straggly beard.

Katie slammed on the brakes.

"I have to go," she told Leblanc, and quickly killed the call.

She peered into the woods, but the face was no longer visible.

Katie got onto the radio to notify the search team.

"I think I saw a man. Someone hiding in the woods. I'm going to check it out," she said. "I'll leave my radio in the car. I'd rather go in quietly."

"Copy that," Bryce said. "We'll keep an eye out. Get back in communication as soon as you can."

Katie stopped the car and climbed out. She pocketed the keys, working on auto pilot, because all her focus was on what lay ahead.

She walked across the empty road. There was a narrow pathway, weaving between the undergrowth. Looking down, she saw clear footprints in the muddy soil. They had been made by heavy boots.

Someone was walking into the woods, and from the size of shoe and length of stride Katie saw in the mud, it was a tall man, walking fast.

She drew her gun, remembering Leblanc's words. She didn't want to trigger the killer and have him jump her when she was unprepared. This pursuit was dangerous enough without that additional level of risk.

Then she moved forward a few steps, walking swiftly but doing her best to stay quiet as she headed deeper into the foliage. Her ears strained to pick up any unusual sounds as she looked left and right, as she peered ahead into the woods, searching for any sign of movement.

The forest was utterly silent, but for the buzzing of insects and the gentle rustle of leaves in the trees.

Eventually, the path led to a small clearing. Katie paused, gripping her gun.

She hadn't seen him yet and had no idea if he had seen her.

If he had, then this part of the forest would be the place he might choose for an ambush. She knew she had to be watchful for that. She perceived him as a desperate man, fearful and cornered, but also a dangerous man who had killed before and would not hesitate to kill again.

Katie moved forward cautiously, all her senses on high alert. And then, she drew in a silent breath as she saw him.

A tall man, pacing ahead on the opposite side of the clearing. His footsteps were almost soundless on the damp, muddy path.

Her eyes narrowed as she saw there was something slung over his shoulder. Moving quickly forward, she thought she picked up a gleam of metal.

Looking more carefully, she confirmed her suspicions. This man was carrying an axe.

She could not afford to let him escape. And at this stage, she didn't care if he saw or heard her. There was going to be a confrontation. She might as well have the element of surprise.

Katie's hand tightened on her firearm, as she broke into a run.

CHAPTER SIXTEEN

Leblanc scanned carefully through the records, perched on a chair in the back office of the Vancouver police department. He felt anxious and pressured and knew his time here was vitally important. He wanted answers. He needed suspects. And he desperately hoped that the next few minutes would turn up some solid leads.

He was looking for men with recent records, who'd offended in the past few years.

Men who had used an axe in their crimes. Men who had attacked women.

And also, men who fitted the vague but essential parameters of height and strength and physical capability that this criminal had clearly shown.

With those guidelines vividly in his mind, Leblanc set out with the search.

He was a fast worker and was familiar with the structure of the Canadian database, which he'd used for two years in Quebec, prior to his employment in the task force. Although he still felt concerned for Katie, he was glad that he'd shouldered this task, to get it done as fast as it could be finished.

Here was something. As he scrolled through the records, his brain on high alert for any of his key words, he found a suspect that fit the parameters.

This had come up near the top of the search, which meant it was a close match.

Speed-reading the file, Leblanc saw this suspect, name of David Fontenot, had been arrested and charged after attacking his girlfriend with a pickaxe. He'd broken her wrist, and had been sentenced to eight years for assault and battery. In the court hearing, he had been described as extremely violent, a man who would not hesitate to use lethal force.

He'd served four years before being paroled last year.

Tapping his fingers on the keyboard to call up more information, Leblanc saw the details were disturbingly similar to the murders committed by the killer they were searching for. From the photos, even the girlfriend fit the killer's parameters. She was in her late twenties, average height, and brunette.

Now, he needed a photo of the man himself. Opening the correct folder, he stared at it intensely.

Fontenot was tall, with a strong build. At the time this photo had been taken, now a few years ago, he had a short, bushy beard.

This was the man Leblanc was looking for. He felt sure of it.

There might be others, but this was without a doubt the strongest suspect, and the one that he now needed to investigate with extreme urgency.

Fontenot's address was on a smallholding twenty miles to the southwest of Vancouver. Leblanc noted that it was very close to the US-Canada border. Without a doubt, it would have been easy for this man to cross the border via the wilderness. He could have traveled to Seattle to commit the other murder.

He was checking all the boxes and now it was time for Leblanc to check him.

Grabbing the keys of his loaned vehicle, he rushed to the door.

*

Half an hour later, after a breathless and speeding drive into the countryside beyond Vancouver, Leblanc pulled up on the dirt road which led to Fontenot's recorded address. He felt resolute that he was going to pin this suspect down and if there was any connection between him and the recent crimes, bring him in.

Here was number three. This was the gate he was looking for.

It was a wire farm gate hanging off its hinges. Leblanc had to climb out to open it, and it rocked and teetered as he carried it to lean against the fence post.

Looking beyond, he saw a trailer parked in front of a small, dilapidated house. There were no other buildings nearby. The area was covered with wild, scrubby grass and bushy trees. But there were footprints in the muddy soil, and a rough path leading to the door that recently had gravel dumped on it. So the place was inhabited and certainly not abandoned.

However, it seemed eerily still, the only sound the hum of the car engine as he sat, watching and listening.

This was clearly the location of a man who lived on his own, who needed his privacy, and again, this tied in with what Katie had deduced about his personality so far.

Drawing his gun, Leblanc climbed out of the car and strode up to the peeling front door.

He knocked hard, and listened carefully.

All he could hear was the thudding of his heart.

"Open up!" he called, knocking again.

No answer.

Leblanc decided to go around the house and check the back. Perhaps he wasn't home. But if he was, he was in hiding and that told Leblanc something.

He knew he would have to be careful, because there was no doubt that Fontenot would be prepared, and might well be armed.

Leblanc's heart was pounding now. He was alert as he circled the house, noting the faded paint, the stained windows, the pieces of wood that lay on the ground, as if someone might have recently chopped some logs. Then his eyes narrowed, and he drew in a breath as he saw the tool that had been used. A big, heavy looking axe, propped up against the wall.

Leblanc was so focused on that axe, that as he passed the door of the trailer, before he could think or react, the worst happened. The door burst open and a tall, powerful-looking, bearded man leaped out with an enraged cry.

Leblanc jumped sideways, whirling around to face him, but the man was too fast and had the element of total surprise. He crashed his body into Leblanc's, throwing him off balance. Then he made a wild grab for Leblanc's gun hand and in the struggle that followed, Leblanc dropped his gun. It tumbled onto the unkempt grass, and then with no weapon, Leblanc found himself fighting for his life.

"Wait! Stop!" he yelled, but with a snarl, Fontenot swung his fist and caught Leblanc in the gut, punching the breath and the words right out of him.

He coughed in pain and his knees buckled, but then he reached out and grabbed the man's beard, twisted it and yanked his head down. His knee came up, hard and fast, slamming into Fontenot's face.

Fontenot dove sideways, avoiding the worst of the blow, yelling in pain.

Leblanc tried to scramble out of the way and make a run to where his weapon lay, but the other man was too quick and too strong. He managed to seize hold of Leblanc's shirt and then, with a furious growl of anger, he flung him against the side of the trailer.

Leblanc ricocheted off it, his head banging against the metal, and for a moment he saw stars and thought he would black out.

But he didn't. Instead, he managed to grab the man again, this time pulling his head down as he threw his own shoulder up. Fontenot grunted as Leblanc's shoulder slammed into his jaw. Then he let go and staggered sideways.

Leblanc turned and dove away, fighting to keep his balance, trying to reach the gun. He needed the damned gun. It could save his life, and against a bigger, stronger, and highly aggressive adversary, he was at a big disadvantage without it. Leblanc had no illusions about the danger he was in if he couldn't get it.

And he didn't get it. Fontenot tackled him from behind even as Leblanc lunged for his weapon. The big man grabbed him and threw himself to the ground, pulling Leblanc with him.

He was yelling wordlessly. His eyes were wild. With a flash of fear, Leblanc wondered if he was completely mad, if he'd lost any semblance of sanity. That was what this fight felt like.

His hands gripped Leblanc's shoulders, and he clamped his knees into the small of Leblanc's back.

Leblanc couldn't move. He tried to throw Fontenot off, but the man rode him down, gripped him tighter.

Fontenot was grasping his neck now, cutting off his air.

Again he tried to throw Fontenot off, but he only succeeded in making the man's grasp tighten.

"Stop it!" he yelled again.

He was strong, too strong. Leblanc could feel his arms weakening. Every second he lay under Fontenot's heavier body, his chances of escape grew slimmer.

Leblanc knew he had only moments left to try and save himself, because if he passed out, it would be the end.

Desperately, with the last of his failing strength, he tried the only plan that he thought might possibly work. If it didn't, it would undoubtedly kill him.

It was a gamble he had to take.

"Police! Stop this! I'm police! I have backup arriving now," he gasped, his voice cracking and barely audible, praying that his words would have an effect and the bluff would work. "If you don't want to get shot by my partner in one minute's time, let me go."

CHAPTER SEVENTEEN

Katie followed the man, her heart banging in her chest, now wishing she did have the radio with her so that she could alert the other police.

It was just her and him, following this track into the depths of the woods, and as she caught sight of him again, as the trees briefly cleared, she saw the shape of the axe clearly.

The sharp, curved blade was distinctive, gleaming dully in the filtered light from overhead.

The crunch of the leaves under his feet was clear and unmistakable. He was a heavy man, and he was moving very quickly.

She had to get closer. She needed to confront him and be sure that he was within range of her gun when she did. She couldn't afford for him to break and run or she might lose him.

Keeping low, moving as swiftly as she could, she doubled her efforts to catch up.

She glimpsed him regularly through the trees. He was striding rapidly now and he was well ahead of her. And the track was taking him deeper and deeper into the woods.

Whatever it took, she was not going to let him get away. She was not!

But then, abruptly, he slowed. She crept forward. Had he reached where he was going? Or was he deciding on a path to follow? She had no idea what he was thinking, but she was sure he hadn't seen her. He was in front of her, standing still, at the edge of a small clearing and was glancing around.

Definitely looking for something.

Or could it be, for someone? Was he tracking another victim, she wondered with a twist of her stomach.

She crept closer, breathless from the pursuit, trying her utmost not to make a sound, but as she reached the trees ahead of the clearing, a small branch cracked beneath her feet and she froze.

"There you are," he called. "I can see you!"

Katie's heart hammered. Had he seen her?

She waited, barely daring to breathe, but through the clustered leaves, she didn't think he was looking her way. So, who was he talking to? She couldn't hear anyone reply.

"It's time," he said, his voice decisive, and she tensed. Katie's heart doubled in speed as, through the leaves, she saw him raise the axe.

What was going on? Did he have another victim there? It sounded as if he'd left someone in the clearing and was now coming back to them.

She had to stop him, because if that axe fell, then who knew what irreversible damage it might do?

"Stop!" she yelled, rushing forward, but her desperate words were too late. As she watched, he brought it down in a rough but practiced arc.

Adrenaline surging, Katie burst out of the clearing.

She needed to get a line of sight on him. Shouting at the top of her voice, desperate to distract him, Katie sprinted toward him, holding her gun.

"Hands in the air!" she yelled.

The man whirled around to face her. She saw the axe in his hands and she saw the fear in his eyes. Beyond him, she saw a black-wrapped bundle lying on the ground.

"Drop it! Drop it! Police!"

He was a big man, dressed in rough clothes, and for a moment, he made no move. What she saw was his stunned expression and the terror in his eyes. He was simply frozen with fear.

A moment later, the axe thudded down into the soil. He raised his arms and backed a step away.

"What is this?" His voice was high, incredulous. "What's going on?"

From behind him, Katie heard another man's voice, and her eyes widened.

"Will! Everything okay there?"

"No! We're in trouble here, Pete. Big trouble. I don't know why."

Another man rushed into the clearing from the other side, stared at Katie in a panic, and put his hands in the air.

Katie moved forward.

"What's that behind you?" she asked. All her attention was focused on that bundle.

"It's – it's my tools, ma'am. And our camping gear. We wrapped them up in a tarp. So they wouldn't get wet or dirty while we worked." He moved toward the bundle.

It was the size and shape of a prone human being, but when he pulled the tarp aside, she saw the green canvas of a tent, and heard the clink of tools.

She still held the gun steady, but she was starting to think there had been a misunderstanding.

"What's your name, sir?" she snapped out.

"Pete Corday," he stammered. "This is my brother, Will."

"What are you doing here?"

"I'm cutting firewood. There's a deadfall tree here. My brother and I are chopping it up."

"Pete, what the hell?" Will sounded as incredulous as his brother. "You didn't tell me we weren't allowed to do this."

With a sigh, Katie lowered her gun.

"We're pursuing a suspect who just killed two people using an axe," she explained. "He fled this way, and I thought it was you. Why were you in such a rush?"

Pete looked horrified.

"It wasn't me, ma'am! We just got to this site. I was rushing because we have a lot to do."

"Do you have proof of your movements earlier today?" Katie asked, calmer now. This had been an unfortunate misunderstanding and she was berating herself for having wasted so much time following him through the woods.

"Proof? I don't know. What proof do you need?" He glanced anxiously at his brother.

"We've been camping nearby, in the campsite on the other side of the road. I can show you that booking, and they can confirm we left the site half an hour ago. There was an attendant at the gate who saw us leave. And we messaged a friend this morning, who's going to come through later and pick up the first load of wood. Can I show you those?"

"That'll do."

With a sigh, Katie moved forward and watched while he scrolled through the phone, showing her the morning's communications with a slightly unsteady hand.

Undoubtedly, these men were here for the genuine purpose of wood chopping.

"Do you do a lot of wood cutting?"

"Yeah. We are here most mornings, looking for deadfalls. We have a network of clients, and supply our neighborhood. It's our little business, as I lost my job at the end of last year."

She nodded. "No problem. Sorry to trouble you. But be careful in these woods. There is a killer on the loose. He's approximately your height, strong, and last we knew, he had a beard. He's dangerous and he could be a threat to anyone he comes across. Stay together and watch your backs. Please, stay alert and do not trust any strangers you meet."

"We will," they promised, looking solemn and appalled.

Katie turned and trudged back the way she'd come, feeling now not only frustrated but also rather embarrassed that she'd pursued such a wrong lead.

But as she walked, she realized that this encounter had, in fact, taught her something important.

Katie thought again of the way Pete had raised the axe. It had been with familiarity, and some practice, but not the level of chilling strength and precision that the killer must have used.

She recalled the crispness of the killing blows, the complete absence of mercy or hesitation. The deadly accuracy.

Whoever this killer was, he was both highly skilled and utterly ruthless.

Until she saw this woodcutter, she hadn't realized exactly how much expertise the killer possessed. And that told her something, she thought, about who he might be. He didn't just use the axe part-time. He was highly proficient at it.

And that meant...

But as Katie's mind drew the strands of logic together, her phone rang. It was Bryce on the line.

"Agent Winter. I know you're not in radio contact, but I need you to meet us on site. We have a breakthrough."

"What? What is it?" she asked, breaking into a jog as she hurried back toward where her car was parked.

"It's the axe. We've found the murder weapon. It's been dumped by the side of a dirt road."

Katie drew in a sharp breath. The murder weapon?

"Are you sure it's the one?" she asked.

"Pretty certain, yes. The blade is covered in blood."

"Send the coordinates. I'll be there as fast as I can."

She cut the call and started running fast. The path was soft and wet underfoot and her feet slipped a couple of times, but she kept going.

Her instinct had been right. The killer had been using the side roads to flee. On the way, he'd gotten rid of the weapon. He was panicking. Discarding his tools. He hadn't even wiped the blade.

With any luck, the axe would hold fingerprints or trace evidence that would point the way to his identity.

CHAPTER EIGHTEEN

Leblanc's muttered words got the reaction he was praying for.

His attacker froze, hesitating. The death-grip on his throat loosened. Leblanc sensed he was looking around, wondering where this backup was, and if he was about to feel a bullet in his own back.

And that gave Leblanc the chance to twist and push, dislodging his attacker and lunging toward the place where his gun lay.

When he was this close to a killer, it was Leblanc's policy to take the offensive, and go for the gun. He'd trained long and hard to be able to make this move, and he was not about to let the opportunity slip away.

He dove for the weapon and managed to catch the barrel in his hand, feeling a sense of vast relief that he was reunited with his weapon. Grabbing the gun, he got the grip into his hand in lightning speed. Then he scooted back, and came up on one knee, aiming it at the other man.

Leblanc could hear the sound of his own breath rasping in his throat. His heart was pounding so hard he could barely hear anything else.

"Don't come any closer. I am a police detective. Put your hands up, now."

With his other hand, he opened his now muddy jacket and flashed his badge.

His attacker froze. He was breathing hard. They stared at each other, briefly silent. Fontenot's eyes widened. He gazed at the gun, the recognition of the threat immediate. He raised his hands slowly.

"You're the police? You're the feds?" Fontenot sounded incredulous, as if he had trouble believing it. But Leblanc could see the fight had ebbed out of him, and he knew he had Fontenot.

"Yes, I am. And who are you?" Most importantly, Leblanc needed to confirm this man's identity.

"Dave. I'm Dave Fontenot."

"Okay, Dave. Do you have an alibi for early this morning? Tell me your movements, and if anyone can confirm them."

"What? Why are you asking this? What are you doing here with these questions?" Fontenot sounded incredulous.

"Tracking a killer. A man who's recently killed three women using an axe."

Fontenot glanced at the axe, propped up against the side of the trailer.

"It wasn't me. I swear it. I had - I had a problem with alcohol a while back. It got the better of me. I did some things I shouldn't have, and served time for them. I've been sober ever since I've come out of jail. I didn't attack anyone."

"You just attacked me!" Leblanc could hear the outrage in his own voice.

"Yeah, I - I thought you were an intruder. Guy on the farm next door, he got his shed broken into a couple days ago and they stole all his tools. I thought this was more of the same. I thought you were coming to rob me. I get suspicious around people. You see, I don't do well with strangers. Never have. It's why I keep to myself, now."

Leblanc nodded. He believed those words well enough. The man's own actions backed them up.

"I've been trying to stay clean. I'm not going back to jail. But I'm also not letting anyone steal my stuff," Fontenot insisted.

Leblanc nodded. There was something strangely honest about his environment and his account of events. Even so, he wasn't going to let this go until he was sure. There was nothing to stop this guy being who he was, and at the same time, moving into serial killer mode when the urge overcame him.

Right now he was down to the bone on leads, and he had to confirm this for sure. Especially since this man had a past history of axe violence. He had a criminal record. And that meant he checked a lot of the boxes they were looking for.

"Your movements this morning," he repeated sternly.

"This morning? Sure. I'll tell you," Fontenot said. "I was working on my truck."

Leblanc looked around. There was absolutely no sign of a truck in this man's house or yard.

An invisible truck? This alibi was not going well.

"What truck?"

"It's at the neighbor's place next door. He keeps it there for me, because he has an undercover place for it, and I don't have that here.

The truck's got a double puncture, because the tires are old. And it's got a leak in the radiator. And one of the front doors has a gap in it. Why the water gets in," he explained.

"Where are your tools?"

"The shed." Fontenot gestured to the small wooden lean-to that adjoined the house. "I built it. It's nothing fancy, but it's solid. I have everything in there. Toolbox and hand tools."

Leblanc stood up and walked over to the door. He opened it and looked in. It was a small shed, built from timber. It smelled of old oil and metal. There was a workbench, some hooks, and a shelf where the toolbox was currently placed.

"So tell me again why you attacked me?" he asked. He was aching all over. He wasn't sure if he believed this alibi. He'd need to speak to the neighbor. And he also wanted a closer look at that axe.

"I've already told you. I was frightened when I saw you. I thought you were a drug dealer, or a robber. I don't want those guys to get me. I'll rather get them first. So I came at you."

Leblanc walked over, keeping a careful eye on Fontenot, and bent down to the axe.

He picked it up after pulling his sleeve over his hand so that there could be no confusion over fingerprints. Then he felt the tip of the blade.

This axe was blunt.

The blade was old and damaged. Leblanc didn't think it could easily cut its way deep into a victim's skull. He was surprised it could even be used to chop wood, and maybe this accounted for the splintered, crooked fragments he saw.

After examining every angle, hoping that he might have found the right suspect, he had to admit that this was not going anywhere conclusive. He didn't think Fontenot was the killer.

"Okay. Give me your neighbor's number," he said. "I'll call him and have a chat to confirm what you've told me here."

"The number? Sure, okay."

Fontenot turned and headed into the house.

A minute later he was out, holding a battered phone. He read the number out to Leblanc.

"He lives further down the road, down the hill. Name's Travis. Please don't tell him what happened here," Fontenot pleaded. "He's a family man. I've tried very hard to keep things good between us."

"Noted," Leblanc said.

"So are you going to charge me?" Fontenot asked Leblanc, now sounding anxious. "Because man, I really didn't know who you were. I wish I hadn't done what I did."

"No. There's no need for that. But next time, my advice to you is to ask questions when someone arrives. Don't go attacking them. Or you really will get into trouble," Leblanc warned.

"Okay. Okay."

"And, if you're worried about someone breaking in, you might consider securing your premises better. I don't even see a lock on that shed. A lock and alarm will protect your possessions, better than jumping on strangers and trying to kill them." He could hear the annoyance in his own voice.

"Right. Okay, sure. Thanks," Fontenot said.

Leblanc got back into his car and started it up, heading back down the road, driving at walking speed over the rutted, muddy bumps, keying the neighbor's number into his phone as he drove.

He felt disappointed that this lead hadn't panned out. All it had done was inflict a beating on him which he thought he hadn't really deserved. He knew he'd have bruises. His arms ached and he had a tender bump on his head where it had bashed into the trailer wall.

But then, just before he dialed the neighbor, his phone rang.

It was Katie.

"Did you find anyone on the database?" she asked.

"I'm triple checking a suspect's alibi, but it's a ninety-nine percent chance he's not our guy," Leblanc said heavily, deciding not to tell her about the physical fight that had played out. "How about your side? Any progress?"

"Yes. We've had a discovery. One of the search party just found the murder weapon. It was dumped alongside a dirt road, nearby a path that runs through the forest. So he definitely was fleeing on foot, but unfortunately he's escaped the search. We're widening the parameters though, and making sure there's a strong police presence at the ferry, and the roads leading to it. I'm convinced he was heading there."

"At least you have the weapon." Leblanc felt excited at the thought the man's identity might soon be known. "Are there any prints on the axe?"

"It's being sent to forensics and they'll examine it for all trace evidence. We're waiting to hear back and hoping it provides us with a lead."

"I hope so too," Leblanc said. "We need to know who this guy is. Otherwise, I feel we're stumbling around in the dark."

"Exactly. I came across someone in the woods, who looked similar to the killer but his alibi checked out. But while I was speaking to him, I had an idea of what we should do next. We need to take another look at the police databases, and do some more research. Shall we meet up at the closest RCMP office, and work together? It would be the one to the east of Vancouver, I think."

"Give me half an hour and I'll be there," Leblanc said, feeling excited to know what Katie had in mind, and more positive that they now had a new direction to explore.

CHAPTER NINETEEN

The music man was hurrying along, keeping to the winding forest paths where the trees provided thick cover. He was alert for any sights or sounds, because he knew he was in danger. Breath was choking in his throat. Scenarios crowded his mind.

Despair and disbelief struggled for supremacy. How had she done that to him? How had she known that he was coming to find her?

It had felt like the end of the world when she'd pulled up in that fancy car to give him a ride. He still felt as if the shock was shuddering through his body. How had she gotten such wheels? Had she killed the driver?

Didn't matter. What mattered was that she was coming for him. And now he had to make an escape. To get to her before she got him.

He could feel the blood freezing in his veins as an image swirled in his mind of her pretty face becoming feral, those white teeth lengthening and sharpening, the eyes becoming narrow and red. She could easily do that, he knew, because she wasn't human anymore. She was a beast.

She could come back from the dead, and he knew she had powers that were beyond his ability to understand. How could he cope with such an adversary?

He'd feared it would happen more than once. He'd known from the moment he'd first seen her again that her powers were beyond his ability to fight. But he'd never expected it to happen again and again, so fast.

This was his fault, and he had to live with it. He'd made the wrong decision. The deadly scenario he was facing now was caused by him alone. She was a monster, but he'd created one.

He felt a sick lurch in his stomach.

Stop it. He had to get a hold of himself. There was no point in agonizing this way. It wouldn't change things, and would only send him into a state of panic from which there was no easy or fast escape.

He could only do what he had done, kill, and flee.

Forcing his mind to follow a logical thought process, the music man considered his actions. He'd dumped the axe. He'd done that for a reason, because he'd started to wonder, superstitiously, if the weapon itself was summoning her back.

He hadn't washed it first. The blade was too dirty, and he hadn't wanted to clean it, to get blood on his hand and clothes. But he'd wiped the handle carefully, knowing where he'd touched it, not wanting any trace of himself left behind. He doubted the police would understand his reasons if they found it. He couldn't let it be traced back to him or then she would have won.

He'd run, after dumping it, run at a speed that had taken him close to the ferry, with his empty guitar case bumping on his back. Drawn in the direction he knew he needed to go, with the brightening sky at his back, he'd headed to the water.

Now, he needed to cross over to get back to her, but he wasn't going on the ferry. He had decided to choose a different route, and avoid it completely.

The music man had a horrible suspicion that they would be checking for him there. That somehow, she'd already managed to convince the police he was a guilty man.

He trusted his own instincts that he should stay away from the ferry, and keep well out of sight. However, to get what he needed, he would have to be around people again.

He felt a chill in his bones at the thought, and shivered, trying his best to calm himself, to keep walking at an even pace, trying to appear relaxed, and without a care in the world.

Originally, he had wondered if he should tell the police what she was doing, but he'd decided against it. The police were dangerous and unpredictable. He couldn't trust them, and was sure they could be fooled by her. They might not believe him. No doubt, she would find a way to convince them he was a killer. He was sure she would have worked it that way.

He stepped up his pace, walking out of the woods and heading down a sloping lane lined with houses. He was almost at his destination. There were a few different points he could have chosen. This one was the first he'd come across and seemed as good as any.

He hoped he would be in time to stop this from happening again. He couldn't bear to see her face, not even once more. He felt the terror stir in his bowels as he wondered how she would kill him. She'd be strong. She could kill him so easily, tear him apart with her bare hands and teeth.

The music man felt suddenly tired. His legs seemed to be heavier than ever. It was hard to move on, to think about what he would do. But he had to plan. He had to think. He couldn't allow himself to panic.

He reached the shore. The smell of the sea was strong. It breezed across, fresh and cool. An early jogger gave him a smile and he felt a thrill of relief that he appeared so normal, despite what he'd been through, despite the fact she was pursuing him so relentlessly.

Down there, by the pier, was a tiny harbor. And in the harbor was a small collection of motorboats.

This was exactly the place he needed, and he was now sure of his next move.

He felt suddenly lightheaded with relief. He wasn't far from his goal now. Without a doubt, someone would have left their boat unsecured. This was a small community, filled with trusting people. And that would give him the ride he needed. It was as if life was pointing the way to him.

The boats were pretty, white and gold, red and blue, looking shiny and clean in the morning's rays.

He bent down and pretended to tie a shoelace, and then looked both ways to see if anyone was coming.

No one.

He stepped into the boatyard, feeling a thrill at his own daring as he heard the cars on the road. He wondered if she was in one of them, behind the wheel, driving, closing in on him again. Pushing back the thought quickly, he hurried across the yard and slipped over the fence.

He walked down to the wooden pier, careful not to slip on the wet planks. He reached the first small motorboat tied to the pier and took a look inside.

There were keys there. He had what he needed.

The music man felt a rush of relief as he leaned over, carefully untying the bowline.

Then he clambered into the boat and untied the stern line. He sat for a moment, thinking about what he had done.

I'm free. I'm free. I'm alive. I'm going to be able to stop her, for good.

He felt like laughing, but that would attract attention.

So he just sat there, breathing a sigh of relief. For a minute, he thought he'd done it. He'd escaped her. Then he heard a noise.

He froze, his hands gripping the boat's edge. He turned his head slowly and felt sick, his heart lodged in his throat. He expected to see her there; he knew his worst fears would be realized and she would be standing and watching him, smiling.

But his heart thudded back down into its normal place as he saw it was an elderly man, heading along the pier in the direction of one of the other boats, carrying a bucket and a cloth.

He nodded at the music man, not seeming to know or care who he was.

The music man nodded back.

He breathed a sigh of relief as he watched the old man walk away. He turned back to the controls, took a deep breath, and then turned the key.

It was time. He couldn't stay. She was coming for him. And he would be ready.

The engine revved and the music man turned the stick, making the boat shudder, and then began to motor away. He opened the throttle and the next moment he was gliding into the water.

He drove the boat, enjoying the freedom and the wind in his face. He felt a burst of exhilaration as he picked up speed across the harbor, heading away from the shore, waiting, hoping she wouldn't show.

He felt a second surge of elation as he turned the boat around, heading out for open water.

Now it was time for the second stage of his plan. He couldn't trust her not to destroy him, so he would have to destroy her first. He didn't understand why this had to be done, but he knew that he had to try. She wasn't human, and she couldn't be saved. She had to be stopped.

When that was finally done, it would be time to stop running, he resolved, feeling the breeze cool in his hair as the boat sped across the water.

When he reached the place he needed, it would be time to prepare.

He was sure that as soon as she realized his intentions, she would be speeding there herself, looking to stop him. But hopefully, before she could reach him, he would have carried out his plans and she would be destroyed, forever.

CHAPTER TWENTY

Katie pulled up outside the RCMP precinct to the southeast of Vancouver. This was where she and Leblanc would be meeting, and where they would embark on the next step of their investigation. She felt confident that this would get them further.

Again, she checked her messages. And finally, there was a report back from the forensic team. She read it eagerly. This had information they could use, for sure. In fact, she couldn't wait to tell Leblanc. It would make their search a whole lot easier.

Then she hurried inside. When Leblanc arrived, they would both use his car, so she could save time by signing this loan vehicle in here.

"Good morning," she greeted the constable at the front desk. "I'm agent Winter, from the cross-border task force. I'd like to sign in one of your cars, and also find out if you have a space where my partner and I could work for a while. We just need a desk and a phone, and access to the databases."

"Sure," the efficient-looking, blonde, female constable said. Then she added curiously, "Is this in connection with the recent series of murders?"

"It is," Katie agreed.

"I'm going to organize one for you right away. Come through," the constable said. "I hope you can solve these. We're literally getting panicked phone calls on an hourly basis from people in the community asking if various areas of the province, or various activities, are safe. And we don't know what to tell them."

"I wish I knew," Katie agreed. "And I sympathize with your predicament. People's sense of safety is so shaken when serial crimes like this occur. We're trying our hardest to move forward with the case. Hopefully, we'll have a conclusion very soon."

"Well, if we're of help in it, I'll be very glad," the constable said gratefully.

Katie followed her down the corridor and into a small side office.

"This is a spare office that doubles as an interview room. It's seldom used. Will it do?"

"It's perfect, thank you."

"I'll bring you some coffee. And you said your partner is joining you?"

"That's right. He should be here any minute."

The constable closed the door and Katie went about setting up her laptop, connecting up to the system, and putting her phone on charge. A minute later, the constable reappeared with a tray of coffee. And also with Leblanc, Katie saw.

"Here you go," she smiled, putting the tray down.

"Appreciate it," Katie thanked her before she left.

Immediately, she noticed Leblanc had muddy streaks on the back of his jacket and a graze on his knuckles. He sat down, looking more harassed than he usually did.

She was about to ask him what had happened, but then decided not to.

Just because a lead hadn't panned out was no guarantee that an investigator would not end up in danger. Especially in the more remote areas, people often didn't like or trust the police. She was sure that he'd ended up in a physical confrontation while checking out the strong suspect he'd gone after.

But that didn't mean he wanted her to know what had gone down. Sometimes, it was a matter of pride.

She controlled her curiosity, deciding to wait until he was ready to tell her.

"So," he said, sitting down opposite her. "What's your idea about this killer?"

Katie quickly gathered her thoughts.

"My feeling is that we've underestimated his expertise with the axe," she said.

"How do you mean?" Leblanc asked.

"When I was searching in the forest, I met up with two men who were cutting firewood. I watched one of them handle the axe. He wasn't expert at it. Looking at the way he handled it, I doubt he could have used it to kill. And this was a man who's been chopping wood for months. He told me he lost his job last year and this is a way of making money."

"And your point is?" Leblanc asked.

He sounded grumpy, and he was shifting uncomfortably in his seat, as if trying to favor a bruise. He was most definitely in a bad mood. She had the sense things really had taken a wrong turn for him earlier, and that his ego, as well as his knuckles, was bruised.

Well, it wasn't like she'd had a perfect outcome in her own investigation. Aiming her gun at an innocent woodcutter had also been rather embarrassing. In fact, she realized with a shock that she didn't really feel ready to tell Leblanc about it. Tracking the wrong suspect for that critical amount of time and then pointing a firearm at the poor man was not one of her finer moments.

All she could take from it was the consolation that it had given her more insight into who the real killer might be.

"I think our guy is a professional woodcutter," she said.

"Like, a lumberjack?" Leblanc asked.

"Yes. I think he's very skilled at what he does. Exceptionally so. It brought it home to me, while watching an amateur at work."

"How do you figure that?" Leblanc asked, his voice challenging.

"From the way he kills," she said. "It's clear he knows how to wield an axe with a huge level of mastery. He knows how to use it with the utmost precision and accuracy. It's extremely difficult to have that level of skill and control and muscle memory. It really reinforced that to me when I was watching the other man today."

"So you think he might have worked for a local firm?"

"Yes. That's exactly what I think."

Leblanc made a face. "But this area is practically the logging capital of the world, isn't it? There must be at least fifty companies of all sizes, in and around Vancouver."

"That's true. But we can narrow it down to a couple of companies."

"How can we do that?"

"The forensic report came back on the axe," Katie told him, watching his eyebrows raise.

"It did? And what did it say?"

"No fingerprints. It was wiped clean. But they identified the axe as a Wetterlings. That's a very particular hand-forged type of axe, that's of extremely high quality. They said they've done some basic research on the brand, and there are only a handful of firms in the area that use this axe, including two of the firms on Vancouver Island. I have a list of the firms."

Leblanc nodded, looking impressed.

"So he might have stolen the axe?"

"Yes. That also gives us a lead. Look, I'm sure tool theft is not unusual in this industry, but again, it narrows down what we're looking for. An employee who left, and shortly afterward, equipment went missing."

"And why Vancouver Island?"

"Because I think he's fleeing there. He was headed for the ferry. I am sure he'll still be trying to get across there. So either he lives there, or else he's familiar with the area, and either way if he's a professional woodcutter, it makes sense that he would have worked there."

"Okay," Leblanc said, dubiously.

"There are a thousand places he could hide. But if we know who he is, and where he worked and lived, it will narrow it down."

Leblanc nodded thoughtfully. "Let's get going then. This does narrow down our search."

Katie felt excited, as well as motivated, that Leblanc was now on her wavelength again.

"So, we're looking for someone who left a logging company in the past few weeks? Who perhaps quit suddenly?" Leblanc asked. "Tools were discovered missing afterward? Or even before. He could have been fired."

"Definitely someone who was problematic or unreliable. Aggressive. And might also have a criminal record in the past," Katie added. "And I don't think we're dealing with an organized person. From what I can tell, he's not preplanning these crimes with any real accuracy."

"True," Leblanc said.

"I mean, most serial killers are careful, attentive to detail. Organized, intuitive, able to work out a plan. They know the direction they're heading in. They're careful to make sure their alibis are in order. They don't make mistakes."

"This guy seems to be winging it, you think?"

"Yes. I don't think he has a clear plan. He seems impulsive. It's due to blind luck that he hasn't made a mistake yet."

"True. If the location or timing of his kills had been slightly different, he might easily have slipped up," Leblanc agreed.

"I don't even know if he's intending to kill or if it's the situations themselves that are triggering him."

"That makes him very unpredictable, then?" Leblanc said.

"Agreed. I think he's very, very dangerous. He's not stable. He's a ticking time bomb."

Leblanc frowned slightly, considering her words. Katie could tell he was taking what she said seriously, and that his mind was leaping ahead as he considered the possibilities it opened up.

"That's why I think he might have shown signs of being unstable, of having psychological problems. Something's happened to create this, and an employer might have taken notice," she continued.

"There you have it. That should give us a good start with profiling," Leblanc agreed. "Now let's get on the phone to these companies, and see if any ex-employees fit these parameters."

CHAPTER TWENTY ONE

Katie often found research to be frustrating, as she was more of a boots on the ground person who loved to head out into action. But now, she found herself excited by the challenging task of identifying the ex-employee who, for some unknown reason, had turned violent and embarked on a killing spree. Without a doubt, research was the best way to follow his trail now.

"The two logging companies on Vancouver Island that use Wetterlings tools are Viceroy Timber and Forest Island Logging. Viceroy Timber is the largest, so shall we start with them?" she asked.

"Yes," Leblanc said. "If you think this person has a record, I'll go back into the criminal database and cross check on that side."

Katie picked up the phone and dialed Viceroy Timber.

"This is FBI agent Katie Winter. I'm busy with a murder investigation, and I need your help."

She was used to the surprised pause that normally occurred after she identified herself on a cold call.

"You do? Sure, how can I help?" the receptionist asked.

"I'm calling to inquire about staff members who have recently left."

"Sure, Agent Winter. If you hold a moment, I'll put you through to our HR manager," the receptionist said.

"Good afternoon," a female voice came on the line almost immediately. "This is Angela Rink. How can I help you?"

"Agent Winter here. I'm working on a murder case and calling to inquire about staff that have left your company recently," Katie said. "Or who might have been dismissed or been subject to disciplinary action. We're looking for fairly specific parameters. Somebody tall and strong. Someone who may have caused trouble in the past or been aggressive with co-workers. And we're also looking for someone who may have stolen tools before he left, or who quit before you noticed theft of tools. Particularly your Wetterlings axees."

"I'll do whatever I can to help." Angela sounded excited. "Let me make sure I'm understanding you. You're looking for information on staff members who have been fired or who have quit in the past few weeks? With the theft of tools possibly involved. Is that correct?"

"That's correct."

"And who might have a history of problems at work, including aggression?"

"Absolutely," Katie said.

"I'll get onto that straight away," Angela said. "I imagine this must be very urgent?"

"Yes. It's extremely urgent."

"I'm going to access the records now, while I'm on the line with you. Unfortunately it's the nature of the business that we do have a very high staff turnover, particularly toward the end of winter when people feel like they've had enough of the cold. And, due to the amount of tool theft we've experienced in the past, we now stipulate that employees purchase their hand tools from us when they start work. We then buy them back when the employee leaves. I don't know if that's something you factored in?"

"I see," Katie said, feeling disappointed. But then, Angela continued.

"I'm going to take a look at the records and see if any of the lumberjacks who recently left us were flagged for any infractions. We do take special note of that. This is an industry where people work long hours together and use machinery and tools that can be dangerous, so we're very vigilant about any issues that could cause harm to co-workers."

"That sounds great, and thank you," Katie said.

Now she was feeling more hopeful.

"Okay," Angela said, after a short pause where she put Katie on hold. "I have three names of employees who were potentially problematic and who left within the last two months."

"Thank you," Katie said.

"The first one," Angela said, after another pause. "Lewis Harrison. He was fired last month for being aggressive toward a co-worker. He attacked him and tried to beat him up."

"Is that so?" Katie raised her eyebrows.

"Yes. The co-worker decided not to press charges, but we would have supported him if he had. At any rate, he was fired instantly. Then the second one is Armin Wenzel."

"Tell me about him?"

"He was a troublemaker. Aggressive to other staff, and unreliable. I see here that he threatened a co-worker with an axe a few weeks ago. He was on his second warning when he quit three weeks ago," she explained. "I'm having a look here, and he didn't return his equipment for a buy back. So he will still have his axe and saw."

"Thank you," Katie said.

"And then there's Samuel Haines. He was fired for being drunk on duty. We don't allow that. Our workers are fired immediately if they test positive on a breathalyzer."

"Thank you very much. Please could you send through the recent contact and address details for these men, and also let me know what areas they worked in when they were on Vancouver Island?"

"I'll do that straight away."

Angela wrote down Katie's email address. Then, after thanking her again, Katie disconnected. She turned to Leblanc.

"I have three possibles. I'm waiting on address details, but do you want to check them on your side before I contact the other company?"

"Sure," Leblanc said. "Pass them over."

Quickly, he tapped in the names.

"Armin Wenzel has a record," he said. "He's the only one of the three that does. He did jail time two years ago after assaulting and injuring another man using a bladed weapon. It doesn't say what weapon here, but it seems to me like we should follow this man up immediately."

"I agree," Katie said. Armin checked all the boxes. He was the man she had in mind, and as she looked at him in the police system, she felt like she'd really narrowed down the search.

He fit the bill in terms of age, height, and physical appearance. And as her email pinged with the address details, Katie saw that he lived in a rural area of Washington State, very close to the Canadian border. Katie was interested by that location, because it was slap-bang in between the two cities where the crimes had been committed. Armin had a criminal record, he was clearly unstable and dangerous, and having worked in the logging industry for years, he would be highly skilled with an axe and would have been in possession of the correct brand of axe when he quit.

He was Katie's top suspect at this point. She knew that she had to go out there, to his current address, and knock on his door.

"I think we should head out there immediately."

"I agree." Leblanc closed down his records. "He's a strong enough possibility to investigate right away. He stands out as being the most likely suspect. And he's also a fairly short drive from where we are now. That address is only about forty minutes away, so it makes sense to go right there. If he doesn't check out, then we can come back here and start again."

Katie stood up from her desk, feeling pleased to be heading out into action again.

"I have a feeling he will check out," she emphasized. "And look at the map, Leblanc. His home is literally a few minutes' drive away from the southernmost ferry point. It's just across the border."

Leblanc raised his eyebrows.

"So he might not have been heading for the ferry after all."

Katie nodded. "We could have misinterpreted his movements. He might just have been trying to get back home, to lay low. Or else, to prepare for our arrival."

She knew that this was likely to be a very dangerous confrontation. Armin might be looking out for the police. There was a strong chance he would become violent and aggressive. In fact, based on his past history, this was practically a certainty. He might feel cornered, and ready to fight his way out.

This was not going to be an easy take down, she knew. They could be walking into a deadly situation, and would need every bit of preparation and planning to ensure that they got their suspect, and made it out alive and unhurt.

CHAPTER TWENTY TWO

Leblanc knew he had to be on high alert for this confrontation. He was not going to go through the same ordeal as he had done with Fontenot, he resolved, as the car bumped along the dirt road which, some miles later, led to Armin Wenzel's cabin.

He'd been too embarrassed to tell Katie what had played out at the previous suspect's place.

He knew she'd seen his knuckles, and the grazes on them. He knew she knew something had happened and that she wasn't saying anything because, partly, she wanted to save his ego.

Leblanc sighed inwardly. That was the problem with a partner that was very much in tune with him. You ended up reading each other's minds, even when it actually wasn't that convenient.

But he was not going to let it happen again. Nor was he going to let Katie get caught up in violence.

This time, Leblanc resolved, he was going to keep a damned hold of his gun, and not let anyone get the jump on him.

They'd crossed the border a few minutes ago and were now heading southwest into Washington State, through terrain that was progressively wilder and more isolated. Right now he and Katie were driving along a dirt road which was little more than two ruts in the earth.

Katie had opened the window a little way, and he breathed in the fragrance of the forest, of pine and damp earth.

"We're on the right track." In the passenger seat, Katie had been keeping a careful watch on the GPS. "It's not far now," she said. "It's in about two hundred yards."

She stared doubtfully around at the isolated terrain, with tracts of thick wood.

Leblanc glanced out of the side window, wincing as a tree root scraped the undercarriage.

"Yes. Looks like a cabin over there."

He slowed. Even though he tried to quell it, he felt nervousness coiling inside him.

What if he'd been wrong in his analysis? What if they'd made a mistake? What if he let Katie down, or messed up in front of his partner? Going into a dangerous take down had so many variables riding along with it, and Leblanc felt like every single one of the possible scenarios was now racing through his mind.

The car bumped over the last stretch of track and he pulled to a stop outside the address where Armin Wenzel was reputed to live.

It was an old, wooden cabin, built in typical style, with an L-shaped porch at the front. It was surrounded by thick woodland, with large trees behind the house.

There was no sign of a vehicle around.

He glanced over at the house, and then over to Katie.

She looked back at him. "Ready?"

Leblanc nodded. "I am."

It was time to move forward. The sooner this confrontation was over with, the better.

"Not many neighbors around," Leblanc observed, as they got out of the car.

"He's a long way from anyone else," Katie agreed in a low voice as they paced toward the house, their feet crunching over stray leaves and twigs.

He knew, uneasily, that approaching a house this way always put them at a disadvantage. For all he knew, through one of those dirty, dusty windows, Armin was already training a gun on them.

If Armin was the killer, he had no history of using a gun and preferred to use an axe. But even that thought was not exactly comforting.

Leblanc drew his own gun. He felt better with his hand around the grip. It was quiet here. Too quiet.

He took a careful step, and then another, his eyes darting from side to side, checking for movement. It didn't take long to cover the distance to the front of the house.

Katie stepped on the porch, her gun held in front of her. She knocked loudly.

"Armin Wenzel," she shouted. "Are you home? Police here. We need to ask you some questions."

There was no response.

Leblanc followed her onto the porch. The silence rang in his ears. Taking a deep breath, Katie rapped again on the door.

101

Finally, with a jump of his heart, Leblanc saw movement from inside the cabin. He picked up heavy footsteps, pacing their way.

Then there was a pause.

Leblanc exchanged a doubtful glance with Katie. What was going on? Was this suspect getting hold of a weapon?

He felt very on edge, and as if whoever was inside was planning something. He didn't want to be met with a gun - or a swinging axe.

They heard a bang and crash from inside. Leblanc jumped slightly, aware of Katie doing the same. Then, with a massive crack, the front door burst open.

Leblanc tensed, springing back and bringing up his gun to aim it at the man flinging the wooden door wide. His heart accelerated.

There was Armin. A big, heavy man with a square, strong face and a bushy beard. He stood in the doorway, filling it with his bulk.

He stared at them in total surprise.

"Sorry, sorry guys. The door sticks in the rain. I've got it wedged from the inside and then have to kick it open."

His eyes widened at the two guns trained on him. Katie lowered her weapon slowly. Leblanc stepped back, but kept his at the ready. He didn't trust any suspects in this case. Armin had a record of violence and Leblanc was going to keep on high alert.

"Armin Wenzel?" he asked, to confirm they had the right guy.

"Yes," the big man said, his eyes flickering from one of them to the other.

"We need to question you in connection with murders that have taken place in recent days, in this state and in Vancouver."

Armin's eyes widened.

"Question me? Is this to do with the woman who was killed in the park, in Seattle? I heard about that. Why me?" He stared at them, seeming honestly perplexed by their presence on his doorstep. "Do you think I can be of help, or what?"

"We've identified that the killer is most likely someone who used to work for a logging firm," Katie explained, her voice hard.

Leblanc watched Armin keenly. To his surprise, the man looked abashed.

"I feel bad. I know I have a past. You probably think it's me, then? I was on a very bad track, a couple months ago."

"Yes, you certainly seem to have been that way," Katie said carefully.

"I went and got help. I'm on meds now. I wish it hadn't taken me so long to get here, get past those hectic ups and downs. Now I'm doing handyman work in the local villages and I've turned over a new page in my book," Armin confessed. "But I'll help you. Or give an alibi if you need one. Do you want to come in?"

Leblanc felt stunned. This was not the outcome he'd expected when they had approached this house. Armin seemed genuinely repentant and he did not seem aggressive.

Even though the man's behavior was surprising, Leblanc knew they must remain cautious.

"Thanks."

Katie headed inside and he followed.

Armin led the way into a simple living room, with a homemade dining room table and a few wicker chairs. It was surprisingly neat and clean. Leblanc breathed in the scent of cooking stew.

"What were your movements early this morning?" Katie asked him as they sat down.

"I was called out at about five-thirty. One of the neighbors got her car stuck in the mud. We managed to pull it out, eventually, and I loaned her my car for the day so it wouldn't happen again. That's why it's not here now," Armin explained. "Then she dropped me off here on her way out, and I worked on some furniture I'm making for someone in the village. I'm doing a table and chairs. Working on it in the shed out back."

"Can you confirm your movements?" Katie asked.

"Sure. Let me show you the messages on my phone from this morning. Here's the whole conversation."

He took his phone from the coffee table, unlocked it, and handed it to Katie.

She read through the messages and Leblanc saw her nod. Clearly, she was happy with their content.

This had been a strong lead, but he wasn't their guy. In fact, Leblanc felt shocked by how cordial the visit had been. Few such outings to speak to suspects in these remote areas were, as his recent experience proved.

"The hiker, Sasha Lee, who disappeared on Vancouver Island last month, is she also part of this? I must say I've been checking the news and wondering what happened to her," Armin said.

Leblanc's eyebrows rose. A missing hiker?

103

Katie shook her head. "Can you fill us in on that? It wasn't part of our case portfolio, so I'm not aware of it, but I'd like to know more."

"She went missing about three weeks ago, while she was on a hiking trip. The weather turned bad and she went off on her own."

Leblanc sat up straighter at that news, as Armin continued.

"Her name is Sasha Lee Arden, and she's actually from this area. She grew up a few miles south of here. The family moved closer into Seattle a couple of years ago, but this community was very torn up about it and we've all been hoping for answers, even though by now we realize that she must have had an accident, fallen down a ravine, something like that. It's sad, though. Not as sad as thinking of her being murdered," he said thoughtfully.

"What does she look like? Her age?" Katie asked.

"Twenty-seven years old. Brown hair, blue eyes, quite a fit girl. I actually met her once, but that was a few years ago now. Here's the Missing poster. I have a copy. This shows you where she was at the time she disappeared."

He took a page out of the desk drawer and handed it to her.

From the gleam in Katie's eyes, Leblanc could see she found this information interesting. Very interesting indeed. In fact, Leblanc could see that Katie was starting to fit puzzle pieces together in her mind.

Coming here had been a stroke of luck, he realized, because it was unlikely that a missing person case would have appeared on their radar when it was already a few weeks old.

But now, he could see that Katie thought there might be parallels with this case, important ones.

And so did he.

"We'll follow up on that. It could be very helpful," Katie told him. "Thank you for your time, Armin."

"No problem," the tall man said.

They stood up and hurried back to the car.

"We need to check the closest logging site to her disappearance," Katie murmured as they climbed inside. "I'm convinced there's a link here. She could have been the killer's first victim, if he was working nearby at the time."

CHAPTER TWENTY THREE

Lily Danford watched the shoreline, strolling to and fro on the sand. It was a cold day, but she thought in her figure-hugging jeans and attractive fur-collared jacket, she was making the most of the weather.

Her boyfriend Doug had gone out on the boat for the afternoon, together with the other couple they were vacationing with.

Lily had stayed behind.

Ostensibly this was to enjoy the shore. She'd also mentioned that the last trip out had made her seasick. But those were not the real reasons.

Lily, in fact, had no desire to go out on the water or even to enjoy the shore, either. She was a city girl through and through, and she didn't care much for the ocean. This trip had been Doug's idea and she'd gone along with it. But then, on the second day, she'd met the man that had made all this worthwhile.

She had stayed behind because she was on the lookout for him. Since the others would be out for the afternoon, she was going to meet up with him and have some fun.

He was a handsome guy. Tall, well built, and with an element of danger about him. He was here practicing for some sporting event and had been as keen as she was for some activity on the side.

It was the second time she'd cheated on Doug, and Lily was so excited that her heart was racing.

She was trying to collect her emotions and keep her cool, but it was difficult. She wondered if she'd end up leaving Doug for him. Of course, that was all part of the adrenaline rush.

The thing was, she was the kind of woman who could be the girlfriend of a top athlete. She was pretty enough, and had a fabulous figure. In fact, given the opportunity, she could be the wife of a top athlete, or of anyone else.

A man like this guy, young, tough, and fit, would want a trophy girlfriend. Lily was a trophy.

And she had been waiting for an opportunity like this. Doug, who was a lawyer, had no time for fun. He was so dull, such a gentleman. Safe and boring.

With this guy, it was a completely different story. He was a hunk, and after their first meet-up the day before yesterday, she'd realized he liked to be in charge in the bedroom. And like her, he was an adrenaline addict who enjoyed the thrill of doing something that was dangerous, but in all the right ways.

Standing on the sand, she stared out at the waves, hoping to see his boat approaching. There was simply nothing more fun and exciting than an affair on vacation. What an experience this was! She'd saved his number as 'John Work' in case Doug saw. And she'd chosen this very isolated spot, where they would not be seen by anyone else.

There! She heard the distinctive sound of a motorboat and shielded her eyes, gazing out to sea. Her heart lodged in her throat. This was him, arriving a little early, but that was all good, since the others had left early. It would give them more time.

She smoothed her hands over her shiny brunette hair, looking forward to what the next few minutes would bring. Lily paced along the sand toward the boat, which was heading for the pier a hundred yards on. Quickly, she walked there, just as he disembarked. She stood waiting, smiling, twirling her fingers through her hair.

He looked to be in a hurry. Then he stared at her, looking appalled.

And she realized with a flush of embarrassment that this was the wrong man.

Seriously, what were the chances of two tall guys arriving at the same rendezvous point by motorboat? It had been an easy mistake to make, if rather embarrassing.

Now that she was closer, she saw this man was taller and heavier. He looked a little older and not as ripped, and the clothing should have clued her in. This old looking black coat was not the type of gear her new lover wore.

If she had worn her glasses she would have seen better, but Lily hadn't wanted to wear them because she thought she looked better without them. But now that she'd gotten close enough to see him clearly, she realized this guy was looking at her strangely.

"You! It's you!" he said.

The wind carried his words to her. She didn't like their tone. This guy clearly thought she was somebody else. And the look in his eyes

106

was - well, it was not normal. In fact, it was slightly unhinged, she thought.

"I don't know what you're talking about!" she retorted.

He flinched at her words. Actually flinched.

Lily stared in wonderment. What was up with this guy? This was sure not turning out the way she'd expected.

"I know you!" he said, his voice high and shaking. "I know you! How did you get here?"

He sounded incredulous.

Lily shook her head. This was turning into a potentially tricky situation, because the guy she was looking out for, aka 'John Work,' could arrive at any moment and she wanted things to go seamlessly, and not for him to find her getting harassed by some creep who looked like a hobo.

"I don't know who you are and I don't care, but I'm waiting for someone else. I suggest you go," she said coldly.

The guy looked at her, and she saw rage flaring in his eyes. "You're lying to me. I know who you are. It's you. And I know why you're here."

She stared at him. "I have no idea what you're talking about."

Then, deciding it would be better not to pursue this, she turned away. She wanted to wait for her lover but if this idiot was going to be hanging around the pier, that was off the cards now. She'd have to message him and tell him to meet her somewhere else. But even that would be a risk since he'd already told her that his girlfriend did look at his phone.

Her assignation had been ruined thanks to this lunatic of a guy, appearing out of nowhere. Now she'd have a battle to see her fit, ripped cutie again. She might not even get the chance.

Stamping her feet in frustration, she turned away from the narrow strip of beach, heading back along the path that led through a bushy, treed area to the chalets on the hillside beyond.

But, as she walked, she heard a disturbing sound.

The heavy thud-thud of footsteps, following her. Her eyes widened and she spun around.

He was pursuing her. He was pounding up the path behind her. His gaze was fixed on her. For a moment Lily stared in sheer, sick disbelief. She could not believe this.

And then, she realized that this was a bad situation. There was nobody on this pathway. There had been nobody at the beach. The man had arrived on his own.

He was deranged, unstable, and he was chasing her. Gulping in a terrified breath, she turned and ran.

She had to get away. Lily ran up the path, dodging in fear between the trees that lined the walkway. She raced along the pathway, hearing the heavy footsteps behind her in the undergrowth.

The running footsteps of a powerful man.

With a chill, she felt that she was running for her life. She had no weapon. She had no way of defending herself. And there was nobody else around, not on this side of the beach. That was why she'd chosen it! Her decisions were coming back to bite her, and now she was being hunted.

"Help me!" she screamed, but the wind tore her voice away. There was nobody close enough to hear her.

The sounds of his footfalls followed her and Lily ran as fast as she could.

She had to get away. She had to escape. She ran on, her heart pounding, her breath catching in her throat. Reaching a fork in the path, she glanced around, at a loss. Then she hurriedly took the path to the right, and ran on.

If she could just make it up the hill, she would be in sight of the street and could call out for help.

But he was so close behind her. She glanced back and screamed again as she saw him just a few feet away.

"You can run all you like," he gasped. "But you won't get away. I won't let you."

Cresting the hill, she saw to her horror that she'd run the wrong way. She hadn't headed toward the road. She'd been racing in the other direction, away from the chalet complex, far out into the wilderness.

Lily felt a fear seize her so terribly; she had never felt anything like it.

Her blood turned to ice. Her legs turned to stone. His hand lashed out, grabbing her shoulder, spinning her around.

She shrieked, but the sound was choked off as his other arm lashed out, grabbing her by the throat, pulling her back against him, his hand clasping her neck in a vice-like grip.

108

Lily was choking for breath, feeling panic so huge that it froze her completely.

To her astonishment, her attacker seemed equally scared.

"You can't be!" he screamed at her. "You can't be!"

Now, finally, she broke free of the paralysis that fear had created. She kicked and fought, but she could not get away, even though she struggled in his arms. He pulled her back against his chest, locking his arms around her.

She couldn't break free. Her attacker had a grip of iron.

She could not breathe. Her lungs were starved of air. Her heart was pounding. Her head was ringing and she struggled again, trying to break free, seeing black spots in front of her eyes.

She heard the sound of his ragged breathing, as he held her tighter, whispering to her.

"You can't be here! How - how did you get here? I d-don't believe this."

He couldn't even speak properly. His words were stammered out in fright.

Lily was yanked sideways as the man reached down. He picked up a heavy branch lying beside the path, as easily as if it were a light twig.

He raised it high.

And then, as he brought it down in a swift, violent arc, she knew nothing more. Darkness engulfed her instantly.

CHAPTER TWENTY FOUR

"I wish we'd known about this missing woman earlier," Katie said. "I feel Sasha Lee might hold the key to this entire sequence of events. Particularly based on the way she looks."

With Leblanc at the wheel, they were driving fast to the closest crossing point. They needed to get to Vancouver Island, and visit Island Forest Logging urgently. Not only was this the logging company closest to the hiker's disappearance, but it also happened to be the other of the two companies that used Wetterlings tools. If only she'd called that company first, Katie berated herself. But she'd had to choose one, and the bigger one was more logical. They'd ended up with what seemed like a solid lead that had required urgent exploring, particularly since the suspect was close by.

In fact, this recent lead had provided an essential missing piece of the puzzle, because Armin had told them about the hiker, so Katie knew she shouldn't be too hard on herself for choosing wrong.

"I hope we can find out more details now," Leblanc said.

Katie got on the phone to Scott as they drove. He answered the call in one ring.

"What's happening?" he said, sounding concerned. "Is there any progress? If you need additional manpower, Clark and Johnson will be available later today. They've just wrapped up a case in Montreal and I can book them on a plane if you need them."

"Scott, we're headed for Vancouver Island and we need to get there as fast as possible."

"Why's that?" he asked.

"We're on our way to the headquarters of one of the logging companies based there, called Island Forest Logging. A few weeks back, a hiker disappeared in the woods, fairly close to this company's operation base. Her name was Sasha Lee Arden. She's still a missing person, and we believe that she might actually be this killer's first victim, somehow triggering this entire event."

"You want me to look up the case for you, also?"

"Please. We need to know everything we can about it."

"I'll organize you transport, first, and then call up the details."

While Katie waited, she stared anxiously at the road ahead. Leblanc was speeding along, driving as fast as he dared. She willed them to go even faster.

The road scrolled ahead of them. Thankfully traffic was light at this hour. Leblanc was taking risks, overtaking at high speed, with his siren on and lights flashing.

Scott got back on the line.

"Okay. Transport is organized. Go to Tsawassen Terminal at Port Roberts. There's a Coast Guard speedboat on standby. They'll take you across to Nanaimo, on Vancouver Island, which is your closest access point to Island Forest Logging. From Nanaimo, I'll ask the RCMP to make a vehicle available."

"Thanks," Katie said.

She caught her breath as Leblanc overtook again, into the path of an oncoming truck. Water misted up from its wheels in clouds.

But Leblanc powered the car safely back into his lane, a moment before the giant vehicle flashed past them.

She could see the crest of the Georgia Strait, the wide body of water that separated British Columbia and Vancouver Island. They were almost there.

"I have information on the case," Scott said, his voice clear and calm.

"Go ahead?" The speed of driving didn't allow for Katie to make notes, but she knew Scott would send everything digitally as soon as he'd briefed them.

"Sasha Lee Arden went over to the island on a Sunday morning, with a girlfriend. They were planning on a day's hike, but the weather turned bad. The friend, Colleen Markham, hurt her ankle and couldn't walk. At that point they were in a mountainous area with no cell coverage. Sasha Lee retraced her steps to try and call for help, but Colleen thinks she got lost and went the wrong way. The weather turned bad, with gale force wind and a snowstorm. In the interim, Colleen found a signal, and was able to call for help and she was rescued."

"And Sasha Lee?"

"She was never found, and her phone went off the network. Colleen thinks the battery died. They all thought that in the bad weather she

111

might have fallen and been injured and so search parties were sent out, but then the weather worsened again, with more wind, and heavy rain."

"Okay," Katie said. She was starting to see why the cross border task force never had this appear on the feed. It had been classed as a hiking accident and nobody had thought that Sasha Lee could have been a victim of crime.

"They resumed the search when they were able to, but her body was never found, and she's still listed as a missing person. Notes on the case conclude that she probably had an unlucky fall and was severely injured and unable to call for help. There are so many remote locations on that island."

"Thanks, Scott," Katie said, feeling glad to have the details.

She cut the call as they arrived at Tsawassen.

Climbing out, they rushed toward the ferry terminal. A uniformed Canadian Coast Guard officer was waiting at the main entrance.

"Winter and Leblanc?" he asked, clearly briefed with their description. "I'm Officer Grady. I'll be taking you over to Nanaimo, and RCMP has a vehicle waiting for you there. If you come with me, we can board the speedboat, and get going straight away."

"Thanks, Officer Grady," Katie said. She breathed a sigh of relief, glad that they had made it this far in the shortest possible time.

Grady escorted them to a small speedboat and helped them both aboard. He started the boat, and headed into the open water, with the boat chopping steadily through the waves.

In the distance, she could see the slim shape of Vancouver Island, with Mount Arrowsmith and the rest of the Coast Mountains beyond. Hopefully, within an hour, they would be at Island Forest Logging, and learn more about the potential suspects who could have caused Sasha Lee's disappearance and triggered this killing spree.

*

Exactly forty-five minutes later, Katie and Leblanc walked up to the front entrance of Island Forest Logging. The timber-fronted office building was located a few miles out of Nanaimo, in a small town called Cassidy.

Already, Katie felt they were in the wilderness. Banks of dark forest surrounded the isolated building, looming into the gloomy sky.

Scott had said that a company representative would be waiting. That would be the anxious looking, forty-something-year-old man in dark pants and a thick jacket, Katie guessed, heading over to him.

"I'm Leo Spillman," he said, offering his hand to her, then Leblanc. "I'm foreman for this operation. I'm pleased to meet you, but what terrible circumstances. We're absolutely shocked that one of our staff might have been involved in this woman's disappearance and other murders."

"It's a very disturbing case," Leblanc agreed.

Katie saw that Spillman was nervous, his eyes darting from side to side.

"We appreciate you taking time from your work to speak to us," Katie told him.

"I've got all the staff records in my office. Please come through. I'm going to do my best to narrow down who it might be. Whatever we can do, we will, but please know we never intentionally hired a criminal. We don't always look at police records, especially for casual staff, but we do keep a careful watch on how our workers behave, and there are strict rules in place."

"That will be fine," Katie said, trying to be reassuring. She liked the fact that he was anxious to cooperate.

They went inside to the small reception area, and from there into a modest side office.

"Please, sit."

Spillman had folders open on his desk. "What exactly are you looking for?" he asked.

"We're looking for any of your staff who would have quit shortly after Sasha Lee disappeared," Katie explained.

He nodded solemnly.

"Unfortunately we did have an entire team who ended their contract the day before. Not all of them had left the premises by then. We give them a day or two to move out, pack up, and so on. But there were a couple of people who resigned and who we had to fire. What are we looking for exactly?"

"Anyone who had problems with violence. Anyone who fought with other employees. You will know who the difficult people were. We're thinking this person may have a criminal record, so if you can narrow down the problematic employees on your side, we'll then cross-check on our side to confirm."

Spillman nodded.

He peered at the computer, tapping keys at a high speed and frowning at his screen.

"There are four people who fit that description. Look, this is a tough, hard industry and we don't expect to hire staff with a completely clean record. But we also don't tolerate behavior that's out of line."

"Understood," Katie said.

"The four men are Gary Saunders, Miles Brand, Adam Watson, and Sam Carter. We fired the first two and the last two quit. Sam Carter walked out one day for no reason, but I do recall that Adam Watson quit under rather strange circumstances. They asked us if anyone would volunteer to help with the search for Sasha Lee. He was one of the fifteen or so people who joined the search on the second day she was missing. But he came back from it early, and he literally walked straight out of the camp site and we never saw him again. Incidentally, there was a break-in in our tool storage area that day, and a few pieces of equipment were stolen. An axe, a saw, and a few other items. We were very busy with people coming and going, and helping out with the search, so we weren't as strict with security as we usually are. Adam Watson was a troublemaker. He was on his final warning. He used to fight with the other men and one of them also said he'd stolen his personal equipment. Boots, and a jacket. They had filed a complaint with us, but before we could follow it up, he walked out."

Katie felt a chill at these words.

"Thanks for your help," she said. "Anyone else who raises red flags?"

"Gary Saunders and Miles Brand were both troublemakers too. But they were fired a week after Sasha Lee disappeared. One for drunkenness, one for non-performance. Both of them went back to the mainland, I believe."

"Do you mind if we have a confidential chat while checking police records?"

"Sure, sure," Spillman said, getting up and leaving the room hastily.

Katie glanced at Leblanc, who was calling up his records.

"I have a match," he said triumphantly. "Adam Watson has a record of violence. It's a few years ago, so he wasn't at the top of my search. But he's now in his thirties and served time in his early twenties for assaulting a woman with an axe." Leblanc sounded eager. "Better still, he lives right here on Vancouver Island. His residential address is in

Westholme, which is about ten miles south of here, and close to the logging operation active at the time. I've also checked the other three that Spillman mentioned, but Adam Watson is the only one with any record."

"We need to go and get him right now," Katie said. Finally, she felt they were closing in on the right suspect.

She and Leblanc headed to the door and rushed out. It would take them less than twenty minutes to get to the small village of Westholme.

In twenty minutes, if they moved fast, they could have the killer in custody.

CHAPTER TWENTY FIVE

Katie kept her gaze fixed on the GPS as Leblanc hurtled toward Westholme. The tires wailed as he took the final corner on the narrow, winding road. The lights and siren were providing a flashing, screaming accompaniment to their drive.

But, as he reached Westholme, Leblanc turned them off. Katie thought that was a wise move. They didn't want to give this killer any warning.

"It's the third house from here," she said.

It felt all the more incongruous that they were driving into a scenic village, with well maintained sidewalks, tall pine trees, and neatly kept homes, with a vista of sweeping mountains beyond. Katie felt perturbed that a killer could be lurking, hiding, and striking, amid such peaceful beauty. It felt very wrong. Hopefully, within a short time, they could make it right.

"This is it." Leblanc braked hard.

Katie surveyed the home. It was a smart-looking cottage, with a well kept lawn. It was surrounded by a low wooden fence, and a timber gate was partway open. They parked on the side of the narrow road and climbed out.

Again, Katie was struck by how peaceful and quiet this small, scenic settlement was. Despite the charming surroundings, she felt her heart hammering as they approached the house and knocked on the door.

They were about to confront the person she suspected was the killer, and she had no idea what would play out, or what level of violence might erupt.

She tensed, hearing footsteps hurry to the door, sharp and regular on wooden floorboards.

The door opened and, to her surprise, she found herself staring at a gray-haired woman.

The woman looked equally surprised.

"Good afternoon. What can I do for you?" she asked.

"We're law enforcement, looking to speak to Adam Watson. We have this as his last known address. Do you know of him?" Katie said.

"I - sure, I do, but why?"

"We need to question him in connection with an investigation," Katie explained.

"Is this – is this in connection with these murders I've been hearing about on the mainland?" she asked. "Surely not. It must be something else, right?"

Leblanc shook his head, his lips pressed together. Clearly, this woman assumed the worst.

"Oh, no." She shook her head, looking shocked. "He's my nephew. I know he's been in trouble in the past. He's been a problem child, that I do know, but he's never stepped out of line here, or done anything wrong. He lodges in my shed. He's just been on a trip out of town. He got back at breakfast time, and is resting up."

"Out of town?" Katie asked, her suspicions hardening.

"Yes. He was in Vancouver for a few days, I think. You should find him home, now. If you go around the back of the house, you'll see the shed."

Clearly not wanting any further part in what played out, she then closed the front door firmly.

Katie and Leblanc exchanged glances.

"We've got our killer," Leblanc muttered.

There was no time to lose in capturing this man. Together, they rushed around the side of the house.

But, as they rounded the corner, they were in time to see a tall, heavily built man in a dark overcoat sprinting away, in the direction of the low, split-pole back fence. With a lurch of her heart, Katie realized that this was Adam, and that he must have overheard his aunt speaking.

Adam vaulted the fence, and sped straight off in the direction of a track leading onto the mountainside.

The door of the shed, which looked to be a tiny, cozy, converted cottage, stood wide open. He hadn't even had time to close it as he fled.

"Stop!" Leblanc shouted, breaking into a run and heading for the fence. He leaped over it and raced after the fleeing suspect.

They could not let this man get away. Not now, not when every interaction with the public increased the risk of triggering further kills.

Katie pounded after him, her heartbeat hammering in her ears.

"Stop!" she called again.

But he seemed to increase his pace at her shouted words, running with the speed of total desperation.

They reached a narrow track winding up into the mountain, and Katie saw him turn hard to the right, his feet skidding on the stones. He was heading toward a stand of dark pines.

Ahead, Katie could see Leblanc was gaining.

As she raced behind them at top speed, Katie tried to judge whether they could catch the suspect before he reached the trees. If he ducked into the woods, they might well lose him. She had no doubt he knew those tracks, where they led, how to double back, and where to run for cover.

Leblanc was closing the gap, but the man was taller, his long legs powering him up the track. Just a few more strides, and he was going to reach the cover he needed.

"Wait! Stop!" Leblanc shouted once more.

"I'll cut him off," Katie called, moving to the left and rushing onto the track. She'd seen another pathway veering around the side of the woods.

Leblanc sprinted ahead, taking the direct route.

Her legs were burning as she forged ahead, her eyes locked on to the man who was still running too far ahead to be caught.

But Katie didn't know if they were going to catch him. He had too much of a lead on them. If he disappeared into the forest, they might lose sight of him completely.

Deciding that some misdirection was in order, she tried another tactic.

"I have a gun. Stop or I'll shoot!" she screamed.

While only a few feet short of the trees, Adam hesitated at her words. He started to turn, as if wanting to check whether this threat was real. And then, his foot caught on a tree root. He stumbled and lost his balance, crashing onto the muddy, uneven ground.

His legs went out from under him, and he slid, headlong, arms flailing.

This was the chance they needed, and they got it. Leblanc leaped forward, wrestling Adam down as he slipped and slithered in the mud, fighting for purchase to get up and run again.

Katie slowed her headlong pace, her boots squelching in the mud. She rushed to help Leblanc, taking a pair of handcuffs off her belt and handing them to him while he held the suspect down.

Adam was shouting, struggling, and trying to fight Leblanc. He was all knees and elbows, kicking and lashing out, gasping out threats, sounding furious.

"I'll get you for this! How dare you chase me!"

Katie grabbed the man's flailing wrists. She was gasping for breath, sobbing for air after the steep uphill pursuit. But they had him.

There was both fear and aggression in Adam's eyes as he looked up at them. Katie noted he had brown hair and a short, scrubby beard.

Leblanc hauled him to his feet.

"You guys will be sorry for this! I didn't do anything!" Adam said, his voice rising and cracking with fear. "Why the hell are you chasing me like this?"

"We'll question you at the police department," Katie told him sternly.

"You can tell us everything under official police interrogation," Leblanc said, clicking the cuffs into place. "Come along with us. Don't give us trouble, and don't try to escape again."

Adam stared at them, wide-eyed and now looking fearful, before Leblanc grasped him firmly by the arm and escorted him down the hill.

*

It was four-thirty in the afternoon, and a light, sleety rain had set in by the time Adam was ready for questioning, stationed in the interview room of the closest RCMP precinct in Nanaimo. He hadn't stopped struggling, and was now cuffed to the chair.

Katie stood outside the room, feeling resolute. They needed this wrapped up. They had to obtain a clear and concise account from Adam.

She'd seen the fear in his eyes as he stared at her on the mountainside. Katie hoped that the questioning would go smoothly, and that she'd be able to use this fear the way she needed it, to get him into the mental state to confess what he'd done.

She and Leblanc had agreed to take turns, so that each could have a different approach. She was going to take the first turn in this desperately important step.

Opening the door, she stepped inside.

Sitting handcuffed at the desk in the small, warm room, Adam had a hostile expression on his face, and he looked at her with wary eyes.

119

She took the seat opposite him, and rested her pad on the desk.

"Let me start by letting you know that we're aware of your criminal past and that you've previously served jail time."

He glowered at her.

"Now, I need to know how you met Sasha Lee Arden, and what happened when you saw her. If you want a photo of her, here's one to refresh your memory. Then we'll move on to the more recent crimes."

Katie opened her iPad and showed him the 'Missing' poster of the pretty young brunette.

Adam's eyes narrowed. His breathing sped up. She was certain his blood pressure was skyrocketing. Without a doubt she saw recognition in his face.

But he kept up a resistant front.

"I don't know who she is," he muttered.

"She's one of the women you killed?" Katie asked, bluntly.

Adam shook his head. "I don't know her."

"You walked out of your job under suspicious circumstances the day after her disappearance. You broke into a storeroom and stole tools. Your story doesn't add up," Katie said, firmly.

Adam shook his head again. "I didn't kill her! And I didn't steal any tools. You're lying. You're trying to get me! I knew it from the moment I saw you. That's what you're doing!" he shouted. He seemed panicked. He was breathing hard. He looked traumatized and totally guilty.

Katie sighed. This fear reaction was what she'd expected, but it was less helpful than she'd hoped.

"I can see you're afraid," she said. "The best thing you can do now, for your own sake, is to tell the truth. Explain to me what happened when you saw her. Were you afraid? If so, why?"

If he'd blotted the actual murder from his mind, she reasoned, then she needed to tease the memory out of him, step by careful step.

He sighed. He lowered his face down for a while, breathing deeply, his forehead pressed on the desk.

Patiently, Katie watched until he raised it again.

"Look, I - I know I need to tell you what happened. But I really, really don't want to get into trouble for it."

His gaze was darting left and right, slippery and elusive. Katie didn't think for a moment she was going to get the truth from him. But at least he looked ready to talk. Once they'd cut through the lies, he would have nowhere left to turn. Then they could increase the pressure.

"It will go much better for you if you tell me," Katie said.

"I joined that search. I wanted to help and - and to look for her. And I found her!"

"You did?" Katie could imagine Leblanc, watching the interview through the mirrored window, and how his dark eyes would narrow at the words.

"I did. She was lying on a path by the ravine. But - but she was already dead. She had a huge gash in her forehead. Most probably, Gary Saunders killed her. He was a violent guy, a psycho. If you could hear how he threatened the other guys when he was drunk, you'd have him sitting here, not me. I didn't do it!"

"You are saying someone else killed her?" Katie stared at him cynically.

Already dead. That was a neat defense, and one she hadn't expected. Adam was trying to wriggle out of this by claiming that this hiker really had died accidentally.

"That's exactly what I'm saying! I - I panicked. Because she was dead. And I knew they might think I did it."

Katie nodded. "Go on?" she encouraged. Now they were getting somewhere. He was talking freely and perhaps the truth would emerge.

"I dragged her body off the side of the trail, and I pushed her into the ravine. I - I was so afraid. But I wanted to hide her. I didn't want anyone to think I might have done this! I don't want to go back to jail."

Katie stared at him, considering what they had so far. It wasn't enough. They needed more details.

"Did she speak to you before you dragged her away? Did she struggle at all? Did she maybe beg, or threaten you?"

She hoped she might get to the reasons why this had been such a devastating episode in terms of Adam's sanity. Something about this encounter had cracked his mental defenses wide open.

"You are not listening!" he raged at her, trying to stand. The desk rattled as he struggled against his ties. "You're not listening to a word I'm telling you! I said she was dead! She was dead when I found her. I know what dead looks like! I didn't want to go down for the crime, so I hid her. And it wasn't me who broke into the tool shed. It was Sam Carter. I saw him that night, after the search. He walked out of the job, and then he came back. He's a weirdo who lives in a fantasy world. He stole an axe and a saw and put them in his guitar case. He calls himself a music man but I've never seen him play any instrument."

Katie sighed. Adam was resisting every step of the way and being thoroughly uncooperative.

But there was one step that she could take to confirm at least part of the story.

If they could find the body, they would at least know that Adam had hidden it. That would take them part of the way. Then, perhaps, they could also ascertain the cause of death. And that might take them another step closer to getting the confession they needed.

"I believe you," she said. It was true enough – she did accept part of his story, but she thought the other part was still untold.

She was surprised by the devastating relief she saw on his face.

"You believe me? You do?" he asked hopefully, his voice quivering.

"We need to confirm your version," she said. "So I'm going to need you to tell me exactly where this body is. Can you describe the location, and where you disposed of Sasha Lee? Because we need to go and find her body, urgently. Then we can take the next step with you."

Adam thought for a moment, frowning.

Then he nodded and Katie felt a flare of triumph.

"I can remember exactly where it was," he said. "If you can bring me a map, I'll show you."

CHAPTER TWENTY SIX

He was back. Finally, the music man was here again.

He tramped over the familiar track that led deep into the forest, close to the camp where he had worked. One last time, he had killed her incarnation. It had been the most powerful one yet, but he'd done it.

Now, it was time to find her. He knew what he had to do. Find her and bury her so that this stopped happening. That was what he had omitted and why everything had gone so very wrong.

But he'd been in a panic. When he'd found her, a couple of weeks ago, she'd been lying, slumped, at the bottom of a rocky slope. He'd picked her up and carried her, hoping to get her to safety. But she'd awakened and had struggled terribly, screaming and kicking.

He'd thought at the time that she'd been badly concussed and that this had been inadvertent behavior, due to her concussion. It was only later he'd realized this was the first sign of the demonic possession that had allowed her to keep coming back from the dead.

In the struggles, he'd dropped her. She'd slipped out of his grasp, fallen down an embankment, and hit her head on a rock.

He'd stared in horror as she lay still, her eyes wide and unseeing, the struggles gone. The deep wound had bled freely for a minute and then stopped.

The music man had turned away, filled with confusion and panic. He'd tried to save her, but he'd killed her. Or had she died just to punish him? He'd felt strange, as if a switch inside his brain, that had been faulty and flickering for a while, had finally failed and gone dead.

Deep within, he'd felt that he'd done something seriously wrong. But he'd been too frightened to confront what he'd done.

He'd known he had to leave, of course, after that. He'd gone straight back to the logging camp, and had called in sick the rest of the day. Then, that night, he'd broken into the tool shed and stolen what he needed. Already, he'd had his plan in mind.

The tools of his trade had been hidden away in his guitar case when he'd run. He already felt paranoid and as if he'd done something unforgivable for which he would be punished. He just hadn't thought that she would be the one to punish him. He'd crossed over into Canada and then headed into the States, not knowing clearly where he was going, but knowing he needed to get away.

But while walking through a park, in the direction of a cheap motel he'd heard about on the city's outskirts, he had seen her again. She'd come back from the dead, and terror had surged inside him.

He'd known there was only one solution. He killed her and fled, only to find she was pursuing him once more, that she was coming back again. Unstoppable. He knew with a terrible fear that her aim was now to destroy him. He'd fled again. She'd followed.

The music man had stayed hidden away, as she'd prowled. Daily, he'd studied the news and read of a crazed killer who had been attacking young women. He'd kept watching the news, wondering who this killer was, and why there were no reports of attacks from the undead, because that was what he'd been looking out for.

He'd kept the axe with him.

He'd been so afraid that she might try to come back to him, to seek him out, and take him over.

Perhaps that was what had happened, he thought. He could have opened up a door to let her possess him.

In desperation he had come to understand that his world was no longer his own. Again and again he'd attempted to defend himself and eventually he'd reached the only conclusion.

He had to go back. He had to find her and bury her.

Now he was on his way.

He trudged up the path he knew so well. On this cold afternoon there was nobody else around. That was good, because he needed to work alone. It had been mostly cold and freezing, but her body might already be in a state of decay. He would have to dig a grave.

He knew there was a spot in this forest where he could do what he needed without being disturbed. With the recent rain the soil was soft. It wouldn't take long, and he could easily cover it and hide it afterward.

He'd come prepared. He'd taken a shovel and a spade from a garden shed he passed, and a roll of plastic sheeting to wrap her body in. Now all he needed was her body.

He headed off into the forest, following his own mental map. Even though he was searching for her, he feared that she, in turn, was searching for him. His heart sped up as he approached the place where he'd left her. He knew exactly where it was, along a little-used track that he thought nobody else knew about.

A right turn here, over the rocky ridge, and then a hairpin bend around the trees. It was such a hidden place. He was glad he'd remembered it.

But, as he approached, his heart began thundering in his chest.

Where was she?

She was not here. Not where he'd left her.

He began to panic. The thought that she might have come back to life, that she might be creeping toward him even now, filled him with terror.

The only thing that had given him peace was to think that he would be able to bury her, but that was now gone. He dropped his bundle of tools, and began to frantically search around.

Was that a cruel trick of his imagination, he wondered, a last-minute betrayal of his mind? Had he forgotten where this scene had played out?

There was no time to think about such things. He knew he had not forgotten. It was she who'd escaped. He had to get rid of her and to do that, he had to find her. Because she was here and would come back for him.

How could this have happened? His mind was in a whirl. He could sense the panic rising in his chest.

"What am I going to do now?" he said, aloud, his voice breathy.

She was close to him, he believed. Probably laughing at his fear. He tried to listen and peer into the forest, to see if he could see her, but he could hear nothing, see nothing.

He began to panic. He searched harder. He searched faster. Storming up and down the track, he began bellowing with frustration and rage.

But eventually he stopped. He stood, with his head in his hands.

She'd outwitted him.

She'd escaped, and was near, waiting to spring on him. He felt a dread, a terror beyond anything he had ever known, because he knew that he would receive no mercy from her.

She would destroy him. So, he had to destroy her first.

He had to wait for her to come back and then he had to kill her. He had to cut her into pieces. And then he had to bury her so that she would never be able to return to haunt him again.

And then, he had to take this a step further. He had to go out into the towns and settlements, looking for any incarnations of her that she'd already made. He had to hunt them down, eradicate them.

If this island was going to be safe, the music man knew he had to be ready to kill again, and again, and again.

CHAPTER TWENTY SEVEN

Katie stared at the mark on the map. Adam was sending them far into the wilderness, in the mountainous areas of the island. This location was remote and difficult to access.

Was this man telling the truth? Or was he just forcing them to waste time on a hunt that would get them nowhere?

She left the interview room. As Katie walked out, she heard rain rattling the window opposite.

This was going to be a cold, inhospitable and threatening trip, and it was already getting dark.

Leblanc walked quickly out of the side room.

"He's lying," he said. "Of course he killed her. But how do we prove it?"

"We have to go and find the body," she said. "We have to check out his story and see if there's any further proof in the body itself. This is all sounding extremely weird to me. It's like a made-up story, but what's bothering me in a different way is how relieved he seemed when I said I believed him. That reaction seemed so genuine."

Leblanc looked less convinced.

"I think he's delusional. He's probably relieved you bought his versions. And this is wasting our time," he said. "We should press charges and get a search party to go and look for the body tomorrow morning."

Katie shook her head doubtfully.

"Leblanc, I'm not comfortable doing that. I'd rather wrap this up. There was something about the way he looked that made me want to know for sure. He could be – he could be protecting an accomplice. Someone else who's still out there," she theorized.

Leblanc was shaking his head.

"Nowhere did he mention an accomplice. He just tried to blame others. And I just don't see how we can take this time," he said. "We're going off to try and find a body on the word of a man who swears he didn't even kill her? It doesn't feel right."

"It doesn't feel right because something is missing. There's a piece of the puzzle still to find. The body can take us further. We have to go and look for her, and see if that can guide us." Katie said. Even though she was trying to sound confident and sure of herself, she was just as full of doubt as he was.

"I think it's our duty to check out this lead," she said.

Leblanc shrugged angrily. "A waste of time," he repeated doggedly.

"Look, our arguing is wasting time now," Katie pointed out. "If we don't go, if we don't check this out now, then we have to wait until morning. There's pressure to close this case. Remember what that constable said. It's affecting the entire community."

Leblanc gave in.

"Okay, let's get going. This doesn't feel right, though," he said.

"I agree with that. But I think it's because there's more going on here than we understand yet. And we need to work out what it is."

Katie walked through to the front desk.

"We need some supplies as we're going into the mountains to check out this suspect's version. What do you have available?" she asked the constable. "A couple of powerful flashlights, some rope, some waterproof gear?"

"Yes. I can put those things together for you. We keep some of that equipment in our store room. I'll just be a minute." She hurried out of the lobby.

While she waited, Katie got on the phone to Scott.

"What's happening there, Winter?" he asked. "Is the suspect ready for processing?"

Katie sighed. If only.

"Not quite," she admitted.

"Why's that?"

"This suspect has given us a version that needs checking out. It's odd, and it doesn't entirely make sense, but we still need to confirm it. He's said he didn't kill Sasha Lee, but hid her body, and he's pointed out a place on the map. So we're heading into the wilderness where the body went missing, to see if he is telling the truth about the last step. If he is, we can try to work back, and look for further proof."

"Alright. Good idea. Let's make sure the case is solid. If you find the body, let me know immediately."

"I will," Katie promised. "We'll send the exact coordinates so you can pick her up and take her into forensics."

128

The constable rushed back to the front desk with a canvas bag.

"Here's the equipment you asked for. Be careful out there, and get back as soon as you can. There's a lot of rain in the forecast, and it makes the footing in those mountains very difficult."

"Thanks. We will be careful."

Katie walked out of the building, into the rain.

The air was cold, sharp, and sweet, and it was getting colder. She could see her breath.

She walked over to the squad car where Leblanc joined her.

Somberly, he keyed in the coordinates.

"The GPS says it's going to take us about thirty minutes to get there," he said. "That's going to get us there just before sunset. And it's going to be tough to search out there once it gets dark."

"We don't have a choice," Katie said. She had an uneasy feeling they were missing something. If Adam's version was correct, then there was an additional factor in play. Someone lurking in the shadows? Surely not. But there was no way of proving it.

They climbed into the car and set off along the road that wound its way via the coastline.

Almost immediately, they left the settled area of the island behind, and the road wound its way into the wilderness. In just a couple of miles, it turned from blacktop into nothing more than a poorly maintained track. They saw some vacation chalets perched on the hillside, but that seemed to be the last outpost of development in this direction, taking them quickly into the wild.

The car bumped and squelched in the increasingly thick mud. There was a moment where the wheels spun, but Leblanc managed to steer out of the thickest part of the mire and they continued on, at a pace as slow as a crawl. Rain gusts were spattering the windshield.

The weather was getting bad, and the terrain was worse. But they had to check out this suspect's version.

With difficulty in the bumping car, Katie checked out the GPS as well as the paper map.

"According to the map, this is where we turn off and go on foot," Katie said. "There's still a couple of miles to cover, but in this weather and this mud, I don't think we can risk the car any further."

"Agreed," Leblanc said.

They climbed out.

Rain was spattering on the car roof and within moments after opening the door, Katie's waterproof jacket was cold and drenched.

She put the map away in a pocket and they walked on, slipping and sliding up the narrow track. As they progressed, the rain clouds darkened, and the wind began to blast through the trees.

By the time they got to the third bend in the track, the sun had disappeared behind the hills and the forest was filling with a dark gloom.

Katie was grateful for the flashlights, which lit up the way in front of them in the gloom, and allowed them to pick their way more safely over the increasingly treacherous ground.

"What do you think the chances are that this body is actually in this place?" Leblanc asked.

Katie was about to answer, but then she caught her breath. She saw something ahead, just beside the track beyond them.

"Leblanc!" she said, turning to grab his arm. "Look."

He stopped, letting out a gasp of surprise.

"Here?" he asked, incredulously.

Without a doubt, they were staring at a body. It was the sprawled form of a woman, slumped face down on the track ahead of them.

But this one was in the wrong place. Completely wrong.

This was two miles short of where Adam had told them Sasha Lee would be, and nowhere near a ravine.

With her heart accelerating, Katie moved closer, desperately trying to make sense of the situation and figure out what had happened here.

She stared down at the woman's brown hair. Her outflung arms. Her blue jacket, and figure-hugging jeans, which were not dirty or muddied or even soaked through.

She saw fresh blood on the big, indented wound in her head.

This was a remote track, but it surely would have been traversed by hikers, or the search party, in the past weeks. And that meant there was only one conclusion to be drawn.

She knelt down and gently grasped the woman's wrist.

It was cold, but rigor mortis had not yet set in.

"Leblanc," she said. "This is not Sasha Lee. This is somebody else. He's killed again."

She stood up, feeling a sense of horror fill her. There was no way that Adam could have made this kill. Not after being at home since breakfast time, and then in the RCMP interrogation room for the past two hours.

The killer was still out there. And Katie was sure he must be going to the selfsame location they were. If she was reading his actions and mindset right, he was heading back to his original killing zone.

This situation had just turned extremely dangerous.

CHAPTER TWENTY EIGHT

Leblanc stared down at the body. Shock resonated through him at the sight. Death was always difficult to take in. This woman had not been killed with an axe. But that was because this killer no longer had an axe in his possession. He'd accidentally come into contact with her along the way, Leblanc guessed, and her appearance had triggered him. Then, he had used whatever he could to kill her.

Perhaps one of those branches lying near the path. That would fit with the type of wound he saw.

Katie had been right to come out here. Her instincts had been one hundred percent correct. He wished she hadn't been right. They were now in an extremely risky predicament, walking straight into the area where the killer was now waiting.

Perhaps he'd also come back looking for Sasha Lee, Leblanc wondered.

Looking beyond where this woman's body lay, he saw deep, large boot prints in the thicker mud. The prints were already starting to fill up with water, but without any doubt, they led on the same track that Katie and Leblanc were going to follow.

"He's ahead of us. And on the same route," he said, pointing to the prints.

"If we turn back, we'll lose him," Katie said. "We don't want to do that. We need to find this killer before he can attack anyone else."

Leblanc could see she was thinking hard.

"We're in an extremely dangerous situation here," she said.

"I know," Leblanc agreed, but Katie shook her head.

"It's worse than you think."

"Why's that?"

"I think - although we can't be sure what played out here - that he was the one who killed Sasha Lee. And in doing so, he suffered some kind of psychotic episode."

"Right?"

"That's why he's been killing people who resemble her. Either he is replaying this again and again in his mind, or else he's believing, for some reason, that he has to keep killing her over and over."

Leblanc felt his eyes widen. Goose bumps crawled down his spine.

"You think?"

"Yes. I think so. Perhaps he's come back to try and dispose of the body. To try and face his own demons. Maybe he planned to bury her, or to do something final, so that in his mind he would be able to overcome the perceived threat."

"Go on?" Leblanc said. This entire conversation was giving him chills.

"The problem is she's not going to be there. Because Adam found her body and he threw it down a ravine."

"So what does that mean?"

"It means he will become extremely dangerous. He might well go on a killing spree. He'll seek out anyone who resembles her, actively hunt them down. Not just kill them if they happen to cross his path. He'll become worse. Much worse. I believe that is what will happen and that is what he'll be tipped into."

"That makes sense," he said. "I don't like it, but it makes sense."

"There's also the possibility," she continued, "that he sees us as being part of the same scenario. That he needs to kill us in order to bring the situation to a close. If we're pursuing him, we are going to be at serious risk. But we can't not go. Once he discovers the body is not there, this man is going to turn into a ticking time bomb. Every woman on this island will be at risk from him. There's no telling how far this psychotic state could take him."

Leblanc stared back the way they had come. He felt a chill slide down his spine.

Whatever way he looked at it, they were in a dire situation.

Either they put themselves at risk, or else each additional hour of delay meant a huge additional risk to the inhabitants of Vancouver Island.

"We need to get backup here. Now," he said.

"Agreed," Katie said.

She got on the phone to Scott.

"We have a situation," she told the task force leader, as Leblanc looked uneasily around them.

"What's that?" he heard Scott's voice crackle in response. Signal was patchy here.

"We've found another body. It's a recent kill. It might be from a day hiker or even a vacationer. But it's impossible that it's Adam's work. The timeline wouldn't have allowed for it."

"Another kill?" Scott sounded incredulous.

"It seems Adam was telling the truth. He hid the body, but he didn't kill Sasha Lee. Someone else did and that killer looks to be going to the same place as us. We have to go after him," Katie said. "All the signs are pointing to this man being about to embark on a spree. If he does that, we might end up with many more deaths before we can stop him."

"I'm going to organize backup to the closest landing point, straight away," Scott said decisively. "I'm going to get a helicopter there, before it gets too wet, as there's a big rainstorm moving in. And as many armed officers as we can get together at short notice. Send me the coordinates of this body. And send me the whereabouts of the other body, according to your suspect in custody. Are you sure it's wise to pursue this now?"

"We have to," Leblanc agreed. Now that he'd understood the scenario, he also realized there was no other option.

"Well, in that case, I need you two to be careful."

"We will be," Katie promised.

She cut the call and stared at Leblanc.

"We have to push forward," she said. "We're both armed. Together, we can take him down. And without a doubt, he's here. So this is our best chance."

"Agreed," Leblanc said. "But we need to be very careful. And no matter what happens, we keep together."

"I second that," Katie said.

Somberly, they stepped around the body and continued along the track, with every step taking them deeper into the mountainous wilderness.

The sky was darkening, as was the trail and bush around them.

The cool, fresh air had turned heavy and oppressive. It was raining steadily, and a thick, suffocating mist was starting to roll down off the mountains.

The presence of the killer felt palpable around them, Leblanc thought warily. His eyes strained as he scanned bushes and the path ahead of them.

134

But the only thing he heard was the sound of their feet tramping through the undergrowth, and the faint rustle of branches above, where the wind was picking up, as the rainstorm began to roll in.

"We're nearly there, according to these coordinates," Katie whispered, taking her phone out of her pocket to check them. While she did, Leblanc kept his gun at the ready, shining his flashlight into the thickening gloom.

Leblanc took a moment to shine his light at the thick undergrowth. He wanted to check what was on their left, in the direction they would come up to the top of the ridge. But the dense bush was so impenetrable that he couldn't see.

He moved forward. And then, from above, he heard a thunderous crack.

Leblanc's heart accelerated. He looked up, to see that a tree at the top of the ridge was leaning sideways, toppling toward them.

The massive tree was plummeting down, directly to where they stood.

"Get out of the way! Katie, quick!" he shouted.

With no time to react further, Leblanc leaped out of the tree's path.

His foot skidded and he slipped.

The bush underneath him was not solid ground, he realized, with a twist of his stomach.

It gave way, and Leblanc tumbled down the steep, rocky slope with a cry, his shoes skidding in mud, his hands clutching vainly for purchase as he fell.

Eventually, in a sprawl of limbs, he landed at the bottom of the ravine. Mud showered onto him. From above, he still heard the crashing of the tree. More mud spattered him and he cowered down, wondering if the tree had been the start of a landslide.

But it seemed not. Finally, the crashing stopped. There was silence apart from the persistent spatter of rain on his waterproof jacket, now ripped and torn.

Leblanc could move all his arms and legs. He wasn't hurt. He still had his gun.

"Katie!" he called, feeling frantic with worry about her.

But only silence, and the spattering rain, answered him.

"Katie!" he shouted once more.

Then, with a gasp, Leblanc sensed a shape nearby.

135

He breathed in a reek of decay as he turned. He looked into wide open eyes and saw sickly pale skin, streaked with mud and wet leaves.

Leblanc realized he'd fallen into the ravine where Sasha Lee's corpse had been dumped.

Here she was, and Leblanc caught his breath as he saw the rotting body. There was a gaping wound on her head, which he could see faintly in the gloom. He couldn't see more of her. The rest of her was covered by mud, hidden in a cold, rocky crevasse.

At least he knew now where she was, and that Adam had been telling the truth when he said he'd disposed of her body here.

Now he needed to get back to safety, and to get a crew down here to take her out.

Hoping that Katie was safe, he dug his hands into the steep slope, but all he succeeded in doing was dislodging mud and rocks. It was going to be a battle to get out. And why wasn't Katie replying?

With a chill, he realized why she might be keeping quiet.

There was a chance that the killer had been on the mountainside, watching for them, and had prepared a trap for them. He might even have sent that tree tumbling down.

In which case, Leblanc realized, he'd better keep quiet and stay low. Because that's what Katie would be doing, knowing that any sound, or even the beam of a flashlight, would alert their hunter.

They were separated. His worst nightmare had occurred.

And now his investigation partner was in serious danger. Leblanc had to get out of this ravine and try to find her. He knew that the killer would be targeting her, believing that if he killed her, he would be able to set all his demons to rest.

CHAPTER TWENTY NINE

Katie tumbled, somersaulting down the muddy slope, unable to stop herself. She was aware of the tree behind her, branches crashing around her, its weight skidding down the path. It was going to crush her unless she was able to get out of the way.

She had only a brief glimpse of the steep drop beneath her. Loose mud and stones cascaded down around her, battering her limbs and her face.

With a quick jerk, she twisted around, reaching out with her hands, trying to break her fall, but all she managed to do, again and again, was slide faster and faster down the muddy slope, which was becoming almost vertical as it descended away from the trail, and onto a steep cliff side.

She hit a protruding tree root. Her leg twisted and she was aware of a sharp pain. Her hands scrabbled for purchase and she managed to grasp the root.

It provided just enough grip to allow her to scramble to the side as she saw the fallen tree sliding toward her.

A branch snagged at her clothing, twigs clawed her face. And then the tree was past, crashing into the ravine far below, while she clung desperately to the root that had saved her.

She looked around her. She'd lost both her gun and her flashlight in the fall. It was almost dark. But she thought she saw the faint outline of a steep track, winding up the mountainside above her.

Leblanc! Where was he? She had to find him. Was he seriously hurt?

But she also knew with a cold, sickening feeling that she was not only the hunter, but also the prey. Thanks to her looks, she was at risk of being targeted by the killer.

Katie pulled herself upward and almost fell back, but she managed to steady herself. She kept crawling up the slope, slowly, so painfully slowly, grabbing at roots and earth, struggling to regain her footing. Her leg was usable, but weak, and the muscle cramped agonizingly when she tried to put weight on it.

The rain was spattering onto the trees, muffling any sound, but she thought she heard a faint cry.

Was that Leblanc?

Her heart leaping, Katie was about to call back when she sensed, rather than saw, movement nearby, from the upper part of the track.

Someone was pacing along it. And she was sure it was not Leblanc. It was too big a shape, too heavy a tread. And he'd been wearing a camouflage waterproof jacket. This person seemed to be clad in black, a darker shape in the gloom.

Fear gripped her heart.

The killer was searching for her.

Down here, she was trapped. She had to climb, but in the opposite direction to which she'd sensed the movement.

As fast and quietly as she could, she scrambled up the slope, praying that she'd be able to get away before he found her. She hugged the side of the steep, mud-slicked path, trying her best to keep out of his sight.

Ahead of her she could see a tree branch, thick and sturdy. She reached out, and grabbed it.

Slowly and carefully she pulled herself upward. Her injured leg was trembling with the strain, but fortunately, the killer was on the opposite side of the track, pacing in the wrong direction for him to see her.

The pain in her leg was excruciating, the muscles screaming in protest with each movement, but she kept going, until at last she was able to reach the top of the ravine.

He was going the wrong way. He looked to be heading down into the opposite side of the ravine. That wasn't where she'd heard Leblanc. Hopefully, he would be safe, and this man would avoid her.

In fact, Katie began to hope that his search might uncover Sasha Lee's body. She had no idea where it was now. The fall had disoriented her. But she was sure he must be close to it.

If he found the body, he would no longer be a threat to the two of them. Not for a while, anyway. His attention would be on burying it, or doing whatever his tortured mind told him to do in order to fight the perceived danger.

And that meant they would have time. Time to regroup and time to find weapons, and to wait for backup to arrive.

The path was tortuously steep but Katie felt encouraged as she scrambled up.

Then, as she reached the top of the ridge, her foot skidded. She clawed at a tree root and caught hold of it, just in time to stop herself from falling.

But she'd reached the ridge. Her injured leg was trembling, her hands and her face were scratched and she'd just realized one shoe was missing.

But she'd done it.

For a moment, she stood there, looking out into the darkness. And then, cutting through the rain, she heard the most welcome sound in the world.

The noise of a helicopter.

Scott's backup had arrived. From the direction of the sound, she guessed it was landing on the narrow beach a mile or two from this site. It was the closest safe landing place and the officers had the coordinates for the two sites.

Help would be on the way. Soon they would have everything they needed. Light, backup, and weapons. They could regroup and hunt down this killer.

Feeling a sense of huge relief, Katie headed along the track, making her way as fast as she could in the direction of the sound.

But, as she did so, in the darkness, she saw a shape ahead of her.

It was tall and hooded. She glimpsed pale skin, blue eyes. A square face and a short brown beard.

Katie froze. Too late, she realized that she'd made a fatal mistake. The killer had doubled back to find her. And she was still weaponless.

He was only a few feet away. She could see his eyes, a flash of white in the darkness. And his teeth.

"There you are," a voice said. It was deep and husky, shaking with fear. "I thought I saw you come this way. You were trying to sneak up on me, weren't you? Why are you doing this to me? Why, why, why?"

He sounded crazed with confusion and fear. Katie knew she had only moments before he snapped, and attacked. Could she reason with him?

"I'm not her," she tried, wondering if she could get through to him, if there was any shred of sanity left within him that would truly hear her voice. "I'm here to help you."

"No, no! Don't speak! Don't speak to me!"

Her voice was making it worse. It was triggering him, she realized in despair.

Then he raised his hand in a violent, desperate move and Katie shrank back as she saw the glint of a blade.

The killer didn't have an axe. But he'd found another weapon along the way. It was a saw, its blade rusty and bent, but it was still sharp enough to cause serious damage with just one blow.

He could kill her with that thing, she realized with a sickening feeling. And he would, she knew. Because he thought she was the final incarnation of Sasha Lee.

This was no time to fight. Not when she was without a weapon and up against a tall, powerful man, carrying a saw, who was both violent and experienced in killing at close quarters. Katie knew she couldn't take him on. Instead, she turned and ran for her life, speeding along the slippery, stony track, heading into the darkness.

Behind her she heard his footsteps, inexorably pounding closer.

CHAPTER THIRTY

Katie fled along the slippery track, knowing she didn't have much time, and that she was being pursued by a taller, stronger adversary who was powered by madness and fear.

She struggled to go faster, but the leg that had been injured in the fall was weak and throbbing with pain and her other foot had no shoe. Stones stabbed into her sole, slowing her down.

She had to get away. But she knew that she was too compromised, and he was gaining on her.

Her injured leg was moving as fast as she could push it, but her pursuer's footsteps were getting closer.

She had to find somewhere to hide, she thought wildly. Up ahead, she saw a bend in the track. She could hear the killer's breathing, the sound of his footsteps, crashing closer.

Katie glanced around as the killer lifted his hand, the saw raised in a deadly arc.

She was not going to let that blade cut into her. There was no time to think. No time to plan.

Katie dove to the side, crashing into the bushes, and above her she heard the scream of metal as the saw snagged on the branches.

The lethal blow had been stopped and she'd avoided it, but only just.

In fact, the saw was stuck. It was now lodged in the network of thick, crisscrossed branches. She had only one moment before he pulled it loose and set off after her again. There was no time to run because he would get her. But this was her chance to do two things.

Firstly, to alert Leblanc to her whereabouts. And secondly, to try and stop this man.

She let out a scream that was so intense and loud, it made her throat burn, and she felt it bounce back from the mountain sides.

The scream echoed around the wilderness and she saw the killer pause, shocked by the sound.

If Leblanc was out there, he'd now know where she was.

Now, before he could get hold of the saw again, it was time to fight. She lunged, flinging herself at him, thudding her fists into his stomach.

He stumbled back, muttering, but he was tough and seemed able to absorb the blows. He grabbed hold of her arm, fingers biting into her flesh. His grip was lethally strong.

"No, no, no," he moaned, his breath labored and his eyes wide with fear.

She didn't know what he was trying to do, but she was determined to fight. She rammed her foot into his leg, but he didn't seem to feel it. He was too crazed with fear to feel pain.

Katie raised a fist, intending to smash it into his face, but he saw her move, and grabbed her other wrist.

Snarling with panic, because now he had both her arms, she tried to pull away but his grasp was too powerful. She kicked out with her uninjured leg, but he was ready for it and dodged the blow. It was a mistake. Her injured leg buckled under her.

He shoved her back and she stumbled and fell down. Desperate, Katie screamed and kicked, trying to fight back, but he was too strong.

He was going to take her, she realized in despair. He was going to choke her, put his hands around her throat, and squeeze.

She did the only thing she could. Katie lunged forward and sank her teeth into the hand that was holding her wrist. He let out a howl of pain and fear, and let go.

But he was still strong, she realized with a jolt of fear. He was still strong enough to swing his hand, the one she'd bitten. He did, with a sweep of his arm. It caught her under the chin, knocking her backwards into the slippery mud.

"No! No! No!" he screamed and then he grabbed her, dragging her towards him, wrapping his arms around her, holding her tightly.

"I'm not going to let you get away. I won't let you get away from me again. No more. No more."

"Let me go!" she yelled, but she was completely trapped in his arms. He was squeezing the breath out of her. The life out of her. She had never known a grip with such ferocious intent, or such terrible fear.

Katie's lungs fought for air. But all the struggles were doing was depleting the oxygen that remained to her.

She felt herself getting weaker. Her lungs burned. Dizziness threatened to engulf her. And then, from behind her, she heard the familiar, welcome voice of her partner.

"Let her go!" Leblanc yelled. She guessed he must be about fifty yards away, and closing in fast. She could hear his running footsteps, pounding toward them.

His voice had been the distraction she needed.

She heard the killer let out a gasp and felt him release his grip for one moment, giving her the chance to wriggle free.

Breath flooded her lungs as she gasped for air. The killer whirled around breathing hard, hissing in fear and anger.

Katie jumped onto him from behind, grabbing his neck and holding on as tightly as she could, trying to choke him just like he'd choked her. Only this man was doubly strong. He wrenched her right arm away. Grimly, she held on with her left.

He'd lost all sense of reason. Katie could see his mind was a whirl of terror. He was disoriented, lost. He was extremely dangerous and all he wanted to do was kill and destroy.

Leblanc stormed up to them and flung himself at the killer, determined to bring him to the ground. His weight was enough. The two men toppled into the mud as Katie writhed away.

The killer had the advantage. He'd gotten Leblanc onto his back. He punched him ferociously in the chest and then began choking the life out of him, just the same way he'd tried to choke her.

Katie knew she had to move as fast as she could, using the only weapon that she had available.

With all the strength she could muster, she grabbed one of the fallen tree branches, lifted it, and brought it down, hard, on his head.

There was a crack of splintering wood. The killer grunted. Then he collapsed to the ground, not moving, but breathing harshly.

Katie kept a knee in his back, pinning him down as Leblanc quickly got the handcuffs on him.

She was gasping for breath. Aching all over. Her leg was on fire. Leblanc got out his phone to call the helicopter crew and Katie leaned against him, feeling as if every ounce of strength had been wrung from her.

"You okay?" she asked.

"I am. Are you?"

"I think so."

Katie let out a sigh of relief. She was bruised and sore. But she wasn't badly hurt.

And at last they had this dangerous, confused, violent man in custody.

Katie was certain that he would end up in a state psychiatric hospital for evaluation. He was completely delusional. His own fear had prompted him to commit these horrific crimes. Hopefully, he would now no longer be a threat to others, or to himself.

"It's over," she said.

"It is," Leblanc agreed.

The two of them were leaning against one another, catching their breath.

They were cold, wet, and exhausted. But they were no longer in danger. They had survived the attack of a killer driven to murder by fear, madness, and delusion.

CHAPTER THIRTY ONE

It was after nine p.m. when Katie and Leblanc had finally finished wrapping up the case. Since it was too late to go back home, and they were both exhausted, Scott had booked them into one of the hotels on Vancouver Island.

The hotel was beautiful. A real vacation place, Katie thought, with free cosmetics and a top quality hairdryer and a large, comfortable bed. But the thing she was most interested in was a shower. Long and hot. She felt chilled to the bone, wet to the skin, and as if the grime and mud were ingrained in her after the battle out there on the mountainside.

She climbed under the shower, washing it all away, feeling the steaming needles cleanse the cold and dirt away, and soothe her aching leg.

She shampooed her hair with the fragrant products, and then stood under the spray, letting the water sluice over her, just happy to breathe, and to be safe.

The man who had caused so much chaos and death was locked up in the hospital. He'd been identified as Sam Carter. He'd been a quiet man and not a troublemaker on the logging site. He had no criminal record. He'd had a guitar, although nobody had ever heard him play it. But when they'd looked up his past, they'd found pointers that could have laid the foundations for his instability.

An abusive, alcoholic father who'd kept illegal drugs, knives and alcohol stashed away in a guitar case. That was probably why Sam had kept the guitar case. A reminder of the abuse, and the baggage he carried.

A neglectful mother who had enabled the abuse.

An older sister who'd disappeared under mysterious circumstances, leaving Sam Carter alone.

Katie thought that he would have snapped eventually. It just so happened he'd done so when he'd come across the hiker. He'd told them that he'd tried to save her, but she'd died, and had kept coming back, over and over again.

He'd been haunted by her. Obsessed with fear and the need to destroy her.

Katie realized she had been lucky. If Leblanc had not arrived in time, and the killer had kept hold of her, he would have finished the job. Sam Carter would have murdered her.

She had survived, and she knew it was because of Leblanc. He'd found her in the dark, following her voice. He'd distracted Carter at exactly the right time. Katie felt intensely grateful for her partner's courage and resourcefulness. She had never had anyone like him on her side.

He was tough, dedicated, and he worked well under pressure. He was smart, and he could think on his feet. He was not afraid to speak his mind or disagree with her. He was a sharp, perceptive investigator, and she was more than a little proud to be working with him.

The question was, what did she feel for him now?

He'd been her partner on this case. Nothing more than that.

Or so she told herself. That was all.

Wasn't it?

Katie dried her hair and dressed quickly, using the last of her spare clothing that she'd packed before leaving. Just as well they were heading home tomorrow. But tonight, she was going to the hotel restaurant, to have dinner with Leblanc.

He'd invited her.

Perhaps it was just to celebrate the conclusion of the case, and the fact that they were safe.

But from the strange sense of anticipation when she thought about that dinner, Katie knew it might be more than that.

There he was now. She heard a knock on the door and hurried over, opening it and stepping outside.

In a black shirt, with his short hair neatly brushed, he looked so different from the mud-streaked, desperate-eyed man who'd risked everything to save her, finding her when he'd heard her scream.

He smiled. "What a day!" he said.

"No kidding," Katie quipped.

"I'm glad you're safe," he said softly.

He leaned forward and kissed her.

Katie's heart accelerated. Of course, this was just a friendly kiss, she told herself, it was just a greeting. Quite normal for a case partner after a tough day.

146

But, as she slid a hand around him, pulling him close, feeling the warmth of his body against hers, she knew it wasn't.

It was something else. She felt the door had been opened. Suddenly, they were more than partners. But how much more, and where this would take her, she didn't know.

*

The morning after next, back in her apartment in Sault Ste. Marie, Katie's phone rang at seven a.m. She was still in bed, and stretched over to answer it, wincing slightly as she hit a bruise.

Her mouth literally fell open when she saw it was her mother on the line.

Her mother? Calling her?

That hadn't happened for more than fifteen years. Katie had thought it would never happen. With a twist of her stomach, she wondered if something was wrong. Were her parents okay?

Quickly she answered.

"Mom?"

"I know it's early. I wanted to speak to you."

"Why? What's up?" Katie quizzed her.

"There's something important I want to say," her mother faltered.

"Mom, what is it? Are you okay? Are you and Dad all right?"

"I'm fine. And your dad is fine. I wanted to tell you something."

"What?" Katie asked.

This was so confusing. Her mother sounded so unsure.

"I know you want to know what happened to Josie. You told me you were trying to find that out," her mother said, in a voice close to a whisper.

"To Josie? Yes," Katie said.

Now she felt doubly shocked. She could not believe her mother was mentioning that name. She'd never thought she'd hear her speak it again, ever. What was going on?

"I want to ask you a favor," her mother said, more firmly now. "I want you to tell me what you find."

"Me? Tell you? But you said -"

"I know. Your father doesn't want to know. He won't discuss it. I don't even know why, or what he might think. But Katie, I do want to

147

know. I can't bear the uncertainty of wondering what happened to her. Please, please, will you keep me in the loop on it?"

"I - I will. Sure, Mom. I promise I will."

"Thank you, Katie. I know you can do it. You're my daughter. I – I – it might be too little, too late to say this, but I love you. I'm sorry about the past years."

The line went dead.

Katie was so stunned, she flopped back down on the bed. Her mother's words warmed her. She loved Katie. She wanted to know – and she trusted Katie to find the truth.

And that might happen sooner than later, she thought. Because Charles Everton would soon be released from solitary. And when he was, Katie would see him again.

Perhaps this time, the ice-cold serial killer would decide to tell her the truth.

EPILOGUE

Two weeks later, Katie walked into the small interview room in Northfields maximum security prison, New York State. This was where she had come face to face with Everton for their last disastrous and unfruitful meeting.

She felt cold with nerves. She'd had a sleepless night wondering what would play out.

Katie had spent most of the night trying to convince herself not to have any hopes or expectations, and that Everton was more than likely just using the request for an interview to taunt her again.

Probably, while in solitary, he'd thought of a few more ways to do that. That was all she could expect. He'd know they wouldn't send him straight back to solitary after his stint there and he could afford to play with her hopes.

Even so, she couldn't help having hopes. They boiled inside her.

Maybe Everton would tell her what she wanted to hear. He might say something to rescue her parents from the terrible purgatory they had suffered.

She'd tried to convince herself that Everton was only capable of lying, and of manipulating the truth. She'd tried to tell herself he was smart and cunning, and he had no reason to tell the truth, and no one to tell it to.

But she couldn't help hoping.

Everton had the power to tell her what happened to Josie. And if he told, she'd be able to piece it together

Maybe he really wanted to tell the truth. And maybe he would.

Here he was! She heard the clank of bolts.

Everton shuffled in. After his stint in solitary, Katie thought he looked paler. His hair was longer, straggly and untidy. But his eyes were still the same, cold and hard.

He walked in between two guards. He was in both handcuffs and leg shackles, the signs of a dangerous prisoner. You never let your guard down around a person like Everton. You never trusted him.

149

Now here she was, doing exactly that. Katie literally felt sick with apprehension.

She knew he could sense how she felt. His cold mind held nothing but cruelty. He would use her weakness and not pander to it. So Katie knew she had to force herself to be strong.

She pressed her lips together, lifted her chin, stared at him coldly. As he sat down, she thought she saw a flash of something unexpected in his eyes.

Respect? If so, it was an emotion she hadn't expected to see.

"Good morning, Ms. Winter," he said.

"Good morning, Everton," she replied calmly.

Then there was silence. She waited. She wasn't going to be the first to speak. She needed him to speak.

She was determined to sit there and wait, to let him talk first.

Everton sat back, his eyes boring into her. Katie looked at him, her expression hard. She felt her heart was going to pound right out of her chest.

"I know what you're thinking," Everton said.

Katie felt sure he did.

"You're thinking you have the upper hand because you have me in here. But you're wrong."

Katie felt her stomach clench.

"W-what do you mean?" she asked, trying to keep her voice steady.

"I'm not the monster here," he said, staring at her with those eyes of a predator. "And I wasn't the monster then, either."

She felt ice water suffuse her. "What do you mean?"

"I saw her on the river bank. She was unconscious." He smiled. It was the most calculating expression Katie had ever seen. "I thought of taking her. But I didn't. I can tell you now, it would not have gone well for her if I had. But I thought she was probably going to die anyway and it wouldn't be worth my while. So I left her there."

He paused.

Katie waited. Was there more? She felt sure there was more.

"Someone else took her. I saw another man go to her and help her, as I watched from my hiding place."

"What?" The word burst from Katie. She couldn't believe what she was hearing.

She instinctively felt that the wisest course would not be to doubt or question him but simply to listen. So she listened, taking in every word, every nuance, as he continued calmly.

"He was a big man with dark, shaggy hair. Looking at him I thought he must be one of those off the grid, survivalist types. I didn't see more. I have no idea what his motives were for taking her. I have no idea if she lived or died. That, I cannot tell you."

So many questions boiled in Katie's mind. Was this the truth? Was he just misleading her and raising her hopes again?

Why had he not said anything at the time? Would it even have helped if he had, she wondered. It might not have helped. She had no idea who this other man was, or how far off the grid he operated.

But this brought a possibility she'd never considered. If Josie had been kidnapped by this man, and he'd managed to get her back to health - she might still be alive.

"That's all I will say," Everton said firmly.

He glanced at the guards, and struggled, with some difficulty because of the leg irons, out of his chair.

"Thank you," Katie said softly, before he turned away. "Thank you for this."

He raised an eyebrow at her.

"I like you, Ms. Winter," he said. "If you'd been one of mine - who knows? I might have spared you, too."

With that, he turned away, leaving Katie's emotions in a maelstrom.

Josie might be alive.

Someone else had taken her.

She believed Everton this time. She thought he was finally putting his cards on the table. Unlike much of what he'd previously said, this account was logical, factual, and had not been evasive. And she, too, felt in her heart that there had been more to what happened, so his words made sense to her.

This put a totally different perspective on that day, and now Katie felt more intent than ever on reopening the case file.

Any one of those witness reports might point the way to the person who had taken her.

*

It was mid-morning, and Leblanc was in his apartment, taking a couple of days off after the case before getting back to work. His phone rang, and grabbing it, he saw it was the call he had been expecting, and waiting for.

It was from his connection in Paris, the one who had said he would call if he had more information on the prisoner Gagnon and who would be responsible for his move.

Scenarios and ideas were already crowding his mind as he answered. He felt desperate to know whose responsibility this would be, and if he would have the chance to influence the decision.

Leblanc knew who his friends in the system were, and who his trusted allies were. There weren't many he would trust with sharing such thoughts. No more than three or four.

He felt extremely nervous at the prospect.

The job offer in Paris was still uppermost in his mind and again as he thought about his two life paths, he felt torn by conflict. What would be best? Which one would take him in the direction he should go?

Would it be better to walk away from trying to influence Gagnon's fate or to get involved and finally get the revenge he sought?

He answered, feeling thoroughly conflicted.

"Leblanc. I have some interesting news."

"Go on?" he said. This was so important! What would it be?

"I have found out who is making the decision about Gagnon and the other prisoners," his ex-colleague said.

Making sure to keep his voice calm, Leblanc asked, "And who is it?"

The other man paused.

"It is a surprising, but yet logical, choice."

"Go on?"

"The responsibility will fall to the new head of department. The one who takes over from our friend in the central Paris precinct who is retiring. He did not have time to consider it fully so it is being carried over."

"I - I see. Thank you."

"No problem. And now, I must go."

The friend quickly disconnected, leaving Leblanc in turmoil. This was a twist he had never, ever expected.

The job was open and he knew that if he did apply for it, he had been told he would be considered as an outstanding prospect. He'd prepared his CV and application but then, after deciding to stay with the task force, he hadn't sent them - yet. But he still could. Applications were still open, although they would be closing soon. There was time to change his mind.

And now, the bombshell.

If he became the new head of department in Paris, then the person responsible for deciding Gagnon's fate - would be him.

Leblanc had only a short time left to think about a decision that would change his life, in so many ways, forever.

NOW AVAILABLE!

FORGET ME
(A Katie Winter FBI Suspense Thriller—Book 6)

FBI Special Agent Katie Winter must cross the border, to the islands between Maine and Nova Scotia, to hunt a serial killer leaving bodies on boats. With Spring coming, the thawing ice reveals too much—including a killer who will stop at nothing to get his next kill.

"Molly Black has written a taut thriller that will keep you on the edge of your seat... I absolutely loved this book and can't wait to read the next book in the series!"
—Reader review for Girl One: Murder

FORGET ME is book #6 in a new series by #1 bestselling mystery and suspense author Molly Black.

FBI Special Agent Katie Winter is no stranger to frigid winters, isolation, and dangerous cases. With her sterling record of hunting down serial killers, she is a fast-rising star in the BAU, and Katie is the natural choice to partner with Canadian law enforcement to track killers across brutal and unforgiving landscapes.

A complex psychological crime thriller full of twists and turns and packed with heart-pounding suspense, the KATIE WINTER mystery series will make you fall in love with a brilliant new female protagonist and keep you turning pages late into the night.

Future books in the series will be available soon.

"I binge read this book. It hooked me in and didn't stop till the last few pages... I look forward to reading more!"
—Reader review for Found You

"I loved this book! Fast-paced plot, great characters and interesting insights into investigating cold cases. I can't wait to read the next book!"
—Reader review for Girl One: Murder

"Very good book... You will feel like you are right there looking for the kidnapper! I know I will be reading more in this series!"
—Reader review for Girl One: Murder

"This is a very well written book and holds your interest from page 1... Definitely looking forward to reading the next one in the series, and hopefully others as well!"
—Reader review for Girl One: Murder

"Wow, I cannot wait for the next in this series. Starts with a bang and just keeps going."
—Reader review for Girl One: Murder

"Well written book with a great plot, one that will keep you up at night. A page turner!"
—Reader review for Girl One: Murder

"A great suspense that keeps you reading... can't wait for the next in this series!"
—Reader review for Found You

"Sooo soo good! There are a few unforeseen twists... I binge read this like I binge watch Netflix. It just sucks you in."
—Reader review for Found You

Molly Black

Bestselling author Molly Black is author of the MAYA GRAY FBI suspense thriller series, comprising nine books (and counting); of the RYLIE WOLF FBI suspense thriller series, comprising six books (and counting); of the TAYLOR SAGE FBI suspense thriller series, comprising three books (and counting); and of the KATIE WINTER FBI suspense thriller series, comprising six books (and counting).

An avid reader and lifelong fan of the mystery and thriller genres, Molly loves to hear from you, so please feel free to visit www.mollyblackauthor.com to learn more and stay in touch.

BOOKS BY MOLLY BLACK

MAYA GRAY MYSTERY SERIES
GIRL ONE: MURDER (Book #1)
GIRL TWO: TAKEN (Book #2)
GIRL THREE: TRAPPED (Book #3)
GIRL FOUR: LURED (Book #4)
GIRL FIVE: BOUND (Book #5)
GIRL SIX: FORSAKEN (Book #6)
GIRL SEVEN: CRAVED (Book #7)
GIRL EIGHT: HUNTED (Book #8)
GIRL NINE: GONE (Book #9)

RYLIE WOLF FBI SUSPENSE THRILLER
FOUND YOU (Book #1)
CAUGHT YOU (Book #2)
SEE YOU (Book #3)
WANT YOU (Book #4)
TAKE YOU (Book #5)
DARE YOU (Book #6)

TAYLOR SAGE FBI SUSPENSE THRILLER
DON'T LOOK (Book #1)
DON'T BREATHE (Book #2)
DON'T RUN (Book #3)

KATIE WINTER FBI SUSPENSE THRILLER
SAVE ME (Book #1)
REACH ME (Book #2)
HIDE ME (Book #3)
BELIEVE ME (Book #4)
HELP ME (Book #5)
FORGET ME (Book #6)

Lightning Source UK Ltd.
Milton Keynes UK
UKHW010254090223
416650UK00002B/385